MY CRUEL LOVER

USA TODAY BESTSELLING AUTHOR

T.L. SMITH

My heart has been broken, torn to shreds.

I'm used to the game of pain.

Basically, I'm acquainted with it.

Some would say I've become immune.

That is ...

... until him.

He's cruel, hard, and everything I should stay away from.

For one, he is my boss.

Second, well, I can't stay away.

But in this game of life, maybe pain is my love.

Or maybe I'm not seeing things clearly.

Because every time his hands touch me, it's anything but cruel.

CHAPTER
1

Beckham

"Please." Her voice is a squeal through the phone. I have to pull it away from my ear, and when I do, I shake my head.

Fuck, why did I even answer?

I never answer.

It must have been a momentary lapse in judgment.

That's the only reason I can think of for my stupidity.

"Rebecca," I guess. She has been messaging

me non-stop all day, asking me to come over tonight. That is *not* going to happen.

"Yes. Why? Do you have someone else?" she squeals.

"I do. Multiple, if I'm being honest. Which I informed you of when I first asked you to drop your dress," I say to her as I drive up to my house.

"Arghhh." Her screech is loud through my car's hands-free phone unit.

"Look, I have to go." With a quick flick, I hang up on her. She automatically tries to call back, but I ignore it. Leaning over the seat, I grab hold of my bottle of whiskey to head inside my apartment building. The doorman opens the door for me as I walk in and takes the keys for my car, which he will park.

I was born into a life of luxury and still live in that lifestyle. I'm in my early twenties and already a multi-millionaire, and well on my way to being a billionaire.

"Sir ..."

Spinning on my heel, I turn to my doorman, Jim, who looks behind me and nods.

As I turn, two arms wrap around my middle. "I'm ready to drop my coat," Rebecca whispers in my ear, her voice sounding like cracked glass ready to puncture my entire being. I clutch the bottle of whiskey in my hand, a little too tightly, and then attempt to pull her hands off of me. When I step back, she's wearing a long coat and sky-high heels.

"Rebecca ..." I start.

She shakes her head and starts to undo the top button of her coat. It's then I see the pink skin and realize she's wearing nothing underneath.

Fuck.

Rebecca flicks her long hair back over her shoulder and holds her fingers at the top of the coat to keep it together. "Let's take this upstairs. You know you want to."

I do.

But I don't.

Confliction takes over, my body reacting to something I don't want.

Rebecca's already attached. She wants me and obviously feels some sort of connection I have no wish to experience, so me taking her upstairs to bend her over would do nothing to help this situation I now find myself in.

I look back to Jim, who's watching us with his eyes widening and his mouth falling open.

"Jim, please escort Rebecca out. She is not welcome here any longer." I look back to Rebecca and smile. "I have work to do, and you need to leave. Please don't come back again." I try to step around her, but she opens her coat and showcases herself to me.

I'm a man, so naturally, I look.

But when I think about it, there is nowhere else to avert my eyes right now as she is all up in my face.

When I look up at her eyes, there's desperation there. Her eyes dart around a little, and she jerkily steps from side to side, then the pained stare has me searching for answers I have no questions for.

"Please go. Do you need me to call you a cab?" I ask.

Rebecca closes her coat quickly, her lips form a straight line, and she thrusts her chest out. "Fuck you, Beckham Harley."

I'm pretty sure that's what she wants me to do. Fuck her that is.

Her heels click-clack as she storms out of the building.

Jim holds the door open for her, and I watch as she leaves.

"Don't allow any women in here. Only my sisters," I tell him before heading toward the elevator that will take me to my apartment and away from the craziness that has just enveloped my life at this moment.

"Yes, sir," he says as I step in.

My phone pings, and when I look down, it's a photograph of my niece, Winter.

Pressing call on her contact, Winter's little voice echoes through my sister's phone. "Uncle, I want to come to yours."

The elevator finally opens on my floor. Stepping off, I quickly pace over to the counter and place my whiskey on top, then look at it longingly.

It's the only thing that helps me sleep.

I can sleep without it, but on the weekends, I need it or should I say want it. Not every weekend, just when I dream of *her*. Paige invades my thoughts when I'm exhausted, and I am helpless to stop the flood of emotions those thoughts inflict on me.

I loved her.

And then she died.

Winter reminds me of her. Her soul is pure and sweet. Much like Paige's was.

"Next week! We will go on a date." I hear Winter sigh, then she replies, "Okay," before Rylee's voice comes through the phone line.

"It's your birthday next week. Twenty-four. Are you excited?"

"No," I grumble.

Because I'm not.

Who wants to be excited about getting older?

"Well, we are. August wants to know if you want steak or burgers."

"Neither. I have to go," I reply, then hang up on her.

Some days are harder than they should be.

Some days, I dream of *her*. And when I do, I wake up drenched in sweat.

As I said, whiskey helps. I don't dream after whiskey. I simply pass out. So I walk over, grab the whiskey and a lowball crystal tumbler.

Sitting on my couch, I press play on my phone. My apartment has speakers installed throughout. Every room you walk into, the music blasts, deafening me, helping me to drown out any unwanted thoughts.

I down a shot.

Those beautiful eyes smile with such ease as she stares at me.

I shoot another shot.

Her hand touches mine, and I feel the spark, the electricity that flies up my arm whenever she touches me.

Another shot down the hatch.

I get lost in it.

One more.

I get lost in her.

I scrub my hand over my face. Fuck, tonight is worse than the other nights. Some nights her memory haunts me more than others. The women, the sex, the booze help to drown it out, but it's always her.

Always her face, I see.

Always lost in her.

Even when we were simply friends.

My head drops back on the couch as her lips come into play.

I would have died a thousand deaths to kiss those lips.

I finish the bottle.

My head is heavy, and when I close my eyes again, it's not her I see.

It's blackness.

Nothing but blackness.

CHAPTER
2

Jacinta

I've been working for the Harley family business now for a few months. I was first assigned to work directly with Beckham, but that changed when his old assistant pushed back her retirement. Beckham, or as we all call him, Mr. Harley, has been working with Gloria since he started. And before that, Gloria was the assistant to his father, who built the company.

Beckham, during his time in charge, has helped the company grow and mature into something that is now, well, massive.

He is a bit of a superstar around here, he and his sister. She is the genius with numbers, while Beckham is the genius regarding business practices. I had heard Beckham wasn't even meant to take over the company and that it was to be Rylee, but then she fell pregnant and refused to take on the heavy workload due to wanting to be with her daughter.

Beckham also lost someone dear to him, which in turn has forced him to change his plans.

The people in the office gossip—a lot.

I try not to listen, but sometimes it's hard. You overhear things even when you are not meant to, as we work in an open space environment, so it is natural to hear voices while we are working.

I walk over to Rylee's office to find Shandy at the door. She is one of the accountants and is also good friends with both Rylee and Beckham.

"Jacinta." Rylee smiles as she sees me.

I once despised everything there was to hate about her.

When I was eighteen, I had thought I'd fallen in love with a man who loved me too. But, to my surprise, he was with another woman, the one standing in front of me. I had that man's baby and left. You see, Anderson has a powerful family, and I knew I had to protect my son at all costs. So, I left and didn't return for five years.

But that's not the kicker of the story.

The real ugly part is I got married in those five years I was away. I did it to change my name and protect myself and my son from Anderson's family finding us. And that man I married, that broken, tortured man whom this town doesn't like, was also in love with Rylee. Rylee was in love with him. I married him. And here she sits, still not hating me.

I think I may love her a little now. Go figure.

"Hey, I'm working for your brother today. Any tips?" I ask. She laughs, and so does Shandy. "What?" I state while staring at both of them.

"He's an asshole to work for. Just don't quit. Okay?" Shandy says, which makes Rylee smile.

"Why do you think my office is at the other end of the building and not next to his?" Rylee adds.

Oh geez, I didn't even think of that.

"I'm sure it will be fine," I tell them.

Well, I hope it will be.

I met Beckham once when I was pregnant over five years ago. He was a good guy. Protective of what he loved but overall nice.

However, people change.

"As long as you keep on believing that..." Shandy pats my shoulder and walks off, muttering, "...that's all that matters."

Taking a step into Rylee's office, I spin around and shut the door behind me, then take a seat in front of her. "Oliver has been asking to see more of August. Would that bother you at all?" I ask. She offers me a sad smile. I didn't want to ask, but Oliver loves August, and he was a father figure in his life for a few years.

"Of course not. Why doesn't he come over for a sleepover? I'm sure Winter would even love it." I bite my lip and glance away. "Jacinta…"

I look back at her with a small smile. "I haven't really had a night away from him. I have no family, and well…" When I had Oliver, August was the only one there for me. But he wasn't Oliver's father, even if he was an amazing man with him.

"Well, all the more reason to. You need alone time too, you know. You need to go out for cocktails or sit in your bath and eat chocolate. Gosh, do whatever the hell you want."

Relief floods me as I stand. Rylee should hate me, but she doesn't. I know why August loves her so much, even why Anderson was so scared to lose her. She's someone you gravitate to, even if you don't want to. She's a naturally lovely person and one I have grown to appreciate so much.

"I should go before Beckham arrives."

Rylee laughs. "Hunny, he's already here. Beckham is the first to arrive and last to leave."

My eyes go wide at her words. "Are you joking?"

She shakes her head. "Nope, but his assistant doesn't usually get here for at least another half an hour, so you showing up early will make a good impression." I stand, nod, and straighten my skirt before I turn to open the door and walk out. "Good luck, Jacinta." I hear her words as I quickly step it to my office.

I changed my name to Mary when I was away, but Rylee refuses to call me that. And, eventually, I went back to my real name.

"I may need it," I say quietly to myself as I walk to the other end of the building where Beckham's office is located. My new desk is situated right outside his door. No one is currently at the desk, and the door to Beckham's office is slightly ajar, so I knock lightly.

"What?" he barks.

Oh, crap! I straighten my spine and push the door open, attempting to give him my confident look. However, angry eyes glance up at me as I stand frozen in the doorway. Shit, maybe this wasn't such a good idea.

"Mr. Harley, just letting you know I'll be at my desk if you need me."

His eyes rake over me, and something passes over them before they turn angry again. "What desk? Who the hell are you?" His hands now rest on the desk in front of him as he watches me, or should I say, assesses me. How can someone be so young and yet so damn intimidating? We are almost the same age, but shit, he knows how to get right under your skin and quickly.

He has a power to him. Even from a distance, I can see it, feel it as it emanates from his whole persona. And when you add on his looks, well, none of that is fair to any self-respecting woman.

I shouldn't care about that though, right?

I'm here to work.

To do a job I am paid to do, nothing more.

"I'm your new assistant."

He looks at me again. "You're fired. Shut my door!"

"I..." No other words leave my mouth.

"Fired. Shut the damn door."

I step back and do as he says, maybe with a little more emphasis than needed, when I hear the bang of its closing, then I stand there unsure of what to do. I've only been here for a few months, and now, well, I'm fired. But for what? I don't understand.

"Just sit down and do your work. He fires Gloria every other day of the week," a man pipes up from across the hall. He pushes his glasses up his nose and saunters off. I look at the chair where I'm meant to be sitting and wonder if it's suicide if I sit down in it.

Shit.

I really need this job.

So I take a chance I'm not going to be escorted from the building anytime soon.

Sitting, I start the computer and arrange the work on my desk. Gloria has left me detailed notes everywhere, which proves to be very helpful. Pity she didn't tell me I would be getting fired on my first day working for *that man*. I breathe out a heavy sigh.

"Gloria." I turn at the sound of that voice.

He yells it again.

Then again.

I stand and step over to his door, contemplating opening it until the door swings open in front of me.

"You," he seethes, then looks past me to my desk and then back to me.

"Yes. What can I get for you, Mr. Harley?" He steps back and slams the door, not answering me.

Well, okay then.

I'm glad I was able to be of assistance!

I take my seat and get back to work.

A few hours later, the door opens again, and Beckham stands there, large and intimidating.

"If you insist on staying..." He breathes out heavily. "Then get my lunch." He shuts the door again with a slam.

Lunch?

Fuck!

What lunch?

My eyes search for the guy who helped me before, but he's not there. I could try to work out what Mr. Harley eats, but I'm afraid he will just fire me again. So, I grab my purse and run down to Rylee's office to find her lost in her work. It takes her a moment to notice me, but when she looks up, she smiles at me.

"What does your brother eat?" I ask.

Her brows scrunch, and she looks at me as if I've lost my mind.

"Eat? For lunch?" she asks. I nod. "He gets his own lunch, usually."

"He ordered me to get him lunch. But there were no instructions as to what."

Rylee offers me a sad smile and rolls her eyes.

"He has a wholemeal sandwich with ham and salad. The shop down below knows his order. It never changes. Just say his name and they will know what to do."

"Thanks." I run off and go straight downstairs. When I arrive at the shop, the line is long, so I keep checking the time to make sure I'm not taking too long. The only problem is, I am. I can't push in front of everyone. They are all in a rush.

Yeah, but will they be fired for taking too long?

As the line slowly moves, I bite my lip. There are at least twenty people in front of me, and they are taking forever. My stomach grumbles, making me realize I haven't eaten either.

It takes another ten minutes before the line moves a few more steps forward.

Suddenly, I notice everyone has stopped. Standing in front of the line is someone who wasn't there before.

His suit is unmissable.

It's immaculate.

Just as he is.

His normally gray eyes darken, and they narrow as he stares me down. I see him take hold of his sandwich and walk toward me. My heart rate picks up, waiting for him to get to me.

"I asked for my food over twenty-minutes ago. Did you get lost?" he seethes, and everyone goes so quiet you could hear a pin drop. "I own this place. You push in to get my food next time. Do you understand?"

I nod. It's the only thing I seem to manage when I am around him. *Where the hell is my backbone, I seem to have lost it.*

"Are you all of a sudden mute, too?" he barks at me.

I flinch, and he shakes his head before he literally stomps off like some sort of petulant child.

The line moves, and I can feel everyone's stare on me as we inch forward. When I finally arrive at the front of the line, the cashier gives me a look of pity, and I find I'm not even hungry anymore.

CHAPTER
3

Beckham

"Do you really have to be such an asshole?" Rylee asks, sitting opposite me, her drink in hand as she watches me. "She's nice. Give her a chance."

"Why are you sending me accolades for this woman," I ask. My attention has now gone from the account I've been working on non-stop. It's one of the biggest accounts in the country, and I am trying to acquire it.

"Do you even know she was an employee here before she got the job with you?" One of her brows slides up. "No, you wouldn't, because you pay no one any attention."

"You're sitting here, are you not?"

She waves me off. "Please. I'm your sister. You can't get rid of me."

"Hurry this conversation along. I need to get back to work."

"It's late, and we're the last two here. You should get a life." Rylee stands and walks toward the door.

"I have a life."

"Something apart from fucking things that have two long legs," she sings as she shuts my door with a click.

I scrub a hand down my face, grunt, and then get back to work.

She's sitting at her desk the next morning. I check my watch to make sure I'm not late. Nope, I'm here at my normal time, before everyone else, so I can get things done before any shit hits the fan.

But no, the woman with chocolate hair sits at her desk, head down, as she studies something on her computer. I silently stalk toward her, stopping in front of her desk to simply glare at her. She doesn't notice me at first. Her eyes reading the screen before she pauses then glances up. I watch as her back straightens, and she turns slowly to face me.

She's beautiful, in a classic way. Her lips are painted red, and she's wearing a red suit jacket with a dark-colored skirt. Her heels are kicked off under her desk, which I noticed.

"Sir," she greets me and offers a smile.

I stare.

Who is this woman?

"What's your name?" I ask.

"Jacinta, sir. We've actually met before." I pause at her words. "I had a round belly then." Her cheeks flush, and she looks away.

"You fucked my sister's ex." Her eyes find mine, her mouth falls open, and she draws her head back quickly but says nothing. "Yes, it was you." I remember her now. "You also married my sister's boyfriend." I click my tongue. "You sure do get around." I turn and walk to my office door. As I grasp the handle, her voice comes loudly from behind me.

"Not that someone like *you* would understand, but ... I had my reasons."

Glancing back to her, she is standing, so I look at her bare feet and let my eyes drag up her legs until I get to her face. She is curved in all the right places. Beautiful. Classically so. I like my ladies with a little more ... spice.

"Someone like me?" I question.

"Yes, someone who has family, money..." She pauses. "Is there anything I can get you this morning?" she asks sweetly, her tone changing, clearly wanting this conversation to be over with.

That makes two of us.

Ignoring her, I head straight into my office and shut the door behind me.

Working all morning, I hear her answer calls from her desk, and when lunchtime rolls around, a small knock comes on the door.

"Yes."

She steps in at my bark, a sandwich in hand, and places it on my desk before she turns to walk back out. Just as she reaches the door, she stops.

"What do you need?"

"Rylee said you're trying to land the Jackpot account?"

"What do you know about that? And Rylee shouldn't be sharing that kind of information with you. If she didn't own half this company, I would fire her ass."

She bites her lip before she continues, "I did some research. It seems the CEO goes out every Friday night to Hogs and Goose. Maybe if you offered him an invitation to meet you there, you could talk to him in person?"

My head tilts to the side as I study her. "Who told you to research them?"

"No one. I simply thought it may help."

I glare at her, and she squirms under my gaze for a moment before she walks out the door.

The sandwich she brought me sits on the desk, but before I touch it, I email the Jackpot CEO asking him to meet me for dinner tonight. He replies within minutes and agrees.

Well, shit.

I've been trying for months to get him to respond, so I guess knowing the place he likes to frequent has helped get me the answer I have wanted to hear.

Standing, I grab my coat and car keys and stop at her desk on my out.

"Jacinta," I say her name this time, and she startles before lifting her eyes to me. "The Jackpot CEO has asked me to bring a date. Be there at six. Don't be late. I hate tardiness." Without giving her a chance to respond, I walk straight to my sister's office.

Shandy sits on the seat opposite her, her feet kicked up on the desk and a milkshake in one hand. I walk straight past her.

"Oh, no hello, lover boy?"

"Didn't I fire you already?" Not looking her way, I continue, "Watch what you say to employees, especially since I don't have the Jackpot account yet. You know I've been trying to land it."

Rylee looks at me, confused.

"Jacinta?" she asks. "She asked what was occupying you so she could help. Did she help?" Rylee asks.

"Just be careful what you share. This company is half yours, remember that."

"She's trying to help you, not take you down," Rylee bites back and turns to look at Shandy.

"Loverboy, who's the latest squeeze? Did you get any photos like I asked you to?"

"No," I snap at her.

"Sounds like you have a stick up your ass that needs to be either wiggled or pulled. Which one is it, lover boy?"

Shandy, despite her annoy qualities, isn't all that bad. I thought about fucking her once, but it turns out she doesn't like cock. Now she's become intertwined in my life without my consent.

The door to the office swings open behind me, and I turn around to see Jacinta standing there. Her cheeks go red, and she rolls her lips between her teeth when she notices me.

"Hey, what's up?" Rylee asks.

Jacinta's eyes lock with mine before moving to Rylee, and it's then I notice the color—hazel, with specs of brown throughout.

"It can wait," Jacinta says, backing out as quickly as she can.

"No, it's fine. What's wrong?" Her eyes flick to me, then to Shandy before they go back to Rylee.

"I don't want to ask, but …" She goes quiet and looks to the floor, then back to Rylee. "Would it be okay if Oliver stayed with you for a while after work?"

I feel Rylee's eyes on me, but she answers as I knew she would, "Of course. Winter is dying for company. Bring him straight over."

Jacinta thanks her and walks out.

When she's gone, Shandy shuts the door, and both sets of eyes lock on mine.

"Why does she need a sitter, brother?" Rylee asks.

"She's attending a dinner with me." My sister's brows rise. "Strictly work. Don't get any ideas. I would never, ever touch that."

I shiver at the thought.

That's a big no.

Shandy gives me some sort of weird look before she averts her eyes, and Rylee offers me a sad smile.

CHAPTER
4

Jacinta

I would never, ever touch that.

I heard him say the words, and as I pull up at the front of August's house, that's all that runs through my mind.

Is there something wrong with me?

How come no one ever loves me?

Why am I so broken?

"Jacinta?" August opens my car door, and I smile at him as I slide out of my car. Oliver gets out next and hugs August's legs. I watch as

Oliver runs off in the yard.

"I'm kind of broken, aren't I?" I ask August, my eyes slowly finding his.

If anyone understands, it will be him.

August went from having the shittiest mother to ending up in prison. Then finding a love he thought he never deserved. Then me.

Oliver runs back and clings to August's leg.

"Jacinta." He shakes his head and looks down at Oliver. "Go inside, buddy. Winter is waiting for you."

Oliver nods and heads into the house. I watch him go and hope I'm raising him right, that I'm not making him feel less worthy than I feel.

Because honestly, I feel like a failure.

I look up at August, into his beautiful, kind eyes. How could anyone see a monster there when all I see is someone who was willing to give me a chance and protect me when no one else would. He may have never loved me, but somewhere along the line, I loved him.

"Thanks for this. Mr. Harley requested I go to a meeting with him tonight, and I can't afford to lose this job." My hand pushes my hair back over my shoulder while August shakes his head.

"Beckham is an ass to work for. Everyone knows it."

"So I've heard," I say. But I thought if I stayed out of his way and did the job I am paid for it wouldn't be such a big issue. I guess I was wrong.

"If you need money, Jacinta, ask. I'm happy to help you and Oliver out, you know this." I look past him and see Rylee at the door. She offers me a wave before she walks back inside. She has a lot of faith in him, and I don't blame her. August is crazy in love with her. All he sees is her. Even when I tried to make him see me, it was only glimpses.

"I don't need money. The work I do pays well. Mr. Harley pays well…" I pause. "It's just harder than I thought it would be."

His hand reaches out, and he touches my shoulder. "Jacinta." His green eyes hold empathy.

I shrug his hand off me. "Don't worry, I'll be fine. Oliver should be okay until I'm back. I don't know what time that will be, though."

"Oliver can stay the night. I have his room still set up. Go. Have a kid-free night. Rylee mentioned you probably need one." His hands slide into his pockets.

"She really is amazing," I say more to myself than anyone else. He knows who I'm talking about right away. "I mean, I knew it." I shrug.

"There isn't anything wrong with you. You know that, right?"

"So I keep telling myself, but somehow, the world keeps showing me otherwise."

"You have bad taste in men, is all." He winks, and it's one of the first times I've seen him joke.

"Happiness looks good on you," I tell him honestly. It's true. It really looks amazing on him. "I have to go. Call me if he needs me, right?" I ask.

August nods and watches as I get back in my car. I glance back to the house, and he offers me a small smile before I drive off.

I didn't know what to wear, but my guess would be anything but casual. And as I get out of the taxi, I see I'm right. I spot Mr. Harley straight away, his suit as immaculate as it is every day. But tonight's is all black, even the undershirt, with gold cufflinks, and somehow that makes him appear even more intimidating.

He doesn't spot me straight away as he's typing away on his phone, oblivious to the world around him. Women walk by. They stop and stare. Hell, I damn well stare. He may be young, but he carries himself well.

My long, purple dress just barely drags on the floor, even with my heels on. I'm short, but luckily for me, I learned to sew and can hem my own dresses. I make my way to where he's standing and stop in front of him.

He doesn't notice.

Hell, and if he does, he doesn't pay me any attention.

Not that I was expecting him to in the first place.

"Mr. Harley." He finally looks up at my voice.

His dark eyes rake over me before they land on mine. "You're late."

"I'm early, actually," I say, smiling. "Should we go in?" I ask.

He looks at his watch as he slides his phone into his pocket. "Yes, the clients haven't arrived yet, thankfully."

I nod, and he opens the door for me.

A quick peer over my shoulder at him, I am surprised when he looks down at me with a frown on his face.

"I was raised with women, Miss Leigh. I know how to open the door for a lady."

"Thank you." I walk ahead.

The hostess looks up, but it's Mr. Harley her eyes land and stay on.

He doesn't even have to say his name. She simply directs him to a private booth and he tells her who he's meeting. She nods and walks off, telling him she will bring a bottle of wine as I pull my seat out to sit across from him.

"Next to me, Miss Leigh. If we plan to land the

Jackpot account, I need you to sit near me so you can steal his full attention."

At his words, I push the seat back in and pull out the one directly next to him. Sitting on it, I have to remember not to let my cheeks redden at being so close to him. That the smell of him is *not* intoxicating. That *he* is *not* intoxicating.

"You drink wine?" he asks.

I have to mentally shake myself out of thinking about him.

"I do," I answer, not looking his way, because if I do, he may see it written all over my face.

"Good. And you should call me Beckham tonight."

As he says those last words, I glance up to two older men who are walking over to the table with the same hostess who seated us. They both smile at me, and those smiles they held vanish when their eyes land on Beckham.

"I see you brought back-up," one of the men says.

I recognize him from my research. He owns most of the company. His name is Adam. While his brother, James, owns a smaller percentage and is the other man who is currently taking a seat opposite me.

"A pretty lady never hurt anybody," Beckham says.

What the hell did he just say? I have to hold back my shock that he called me pretty. When I look at him, he offers me a smile, but I can tell instantly it's fake. It still makes something in my stomach flutter though, even if I don't know what.

"No, I guess you're right," Adam relays as the waitress brings over two bottles of wine.

"We would like one of every starter," Beckham announces.

The waitress, who can't seem to look anywhere else but Beckham, nods before she walks away.

"So, you want our business?" James states as he pours himself a glass, but it's more a question than a statement. He offers me one, and I smile and nod my head before he pours mine. "Tell me... sorry, what is your name?" James looks at me.

"Jacinta," I reply with a smile.

"Yes, Jacinta." He's kind, with gentle eyes. "Tell me... is Beckham as lethal to work with as I have heard?" I feel all sets of eyes fall on me. I could tell the truth that he's as ruthless as he is a major asshole. Instead, I try to come up with something positive to say, and that's damn hard.

"I've gained great knowledge working with him. Beckham is dedicated to his work."

James's lip lifts. "Are you choosing not to answer that question?"

"Oh no, he's a delight." And that lie tastes sour on my tongue, so much so I almost pucker my lips with the acidity.

The brothers share a look, and I feel Beckham's eyes boring into the side of my head. When I turn to confirm this, he offers me a smile, and once again, it's fake. It says *you will pay for this* before he turns back to the brothers.

"I'm not going to deny you're the best, Beckham. We all know this. The whole city knows this. But we also only want to work with people we can trust. Can we trust you?"

Beckham's hand comes up on the table, and he taps it lightly.

"You can trust me with your money. Of this, I have no doubt. But as a person, you would have to get to know me. I'm not a complicated man, but I keep my circle small because trusting the wrong people seems to have burned me in the past."

Both brothers nod as they take in Beckham's words while our waitress places our starters in the middle of the table before she walks away.

"Tell us something... something you have told no one else."

Beckham's fingers start to tap on the table, and I can feel his leg bouncing near mine in agitation. "The love of my life died almost six years ago. Some nights when she invades my thoughts, the only thing I can do is drink to drown her out."

The table goes silent.

I go silent.

Holy shit.

I wonder if that tidbit of information is real.

It has to be, right?

That's not something you make up out of nowhere.

"I'm sorry for your loss, Beckham. My wife died over ten years ago, and still to this day, I miss her like crazy," Adam says.

"Yes, sorry. Thank you for sharing that with us," James adds.

For the rest of dinner, the only thing that's spoken about is their business and what Beckham can do for them. Toward the end, and only two wines in, I stand as we get ready to leave.

"It was a pleasure to meet you, Jacinta. I hope at our next meeting we will see your beautiful face."

"I hope so, too." We linger as they walk out, and when they're gone, I reach for my purse and turn to face Beckham.

"Don't be late Monday," he barks at me before he walks off.

Well, okay then.

Guess I make my way home on my own!

Beckham, the asshole, still exists.

CHAPTER
5

Beckham

The weekend was heavy. I stayed in my apartment and didn't leave. Why did I share my most painful secret with them? I shouldn't have shared that. But I also knew it would get me the deal I wanted. And I was right. I landed the deal of a lifetime.

Even if I exposed myself in ways I would never usually do, and even if she was sitting right next to me. Now she knows too.

As soon as I walk into the office on Monday, I find Jacinta already at her desk, headphones on.

When she sees me, she pulls them off and trains her gaze on me.

"Don't you have a kid?"

She was pregnant, this much I remember. She asked Rylee to babysit, which would make me think she's raising the kid by herself.

"Yes."

"So why are you here and not getting him ready for school?"

"Because you're here," she replies.

"I own the company. You are just an employee. Stop coming in so early." Before I get a chance to walk away, her glare could pierce my skin. Once I get to my door, I turn back to look at her, and her shoulders are slumped. "Who has your son right now?"

She twists her hair in her ponytail, flicking it over her shoulder. "I hire a sitter for the mornings."

"How much?" I ask.

She screws up her nose. "Sorry?"

"How much does she charge you?"

"Twenty an hour," she replies.

"I'll be sure to tell accounts to pay you for her cost." I step into my office as I hear her yell out, "You don't have to do that."

I don't reply.

She's a single mother, and every penny counts.

Plus, she seems to be good at her job.

Even if I'm *not* that fond of her.

"Sir." I look up to see Jacinta at my door, a sandwich in her hand and a soft smile on her face. "I got your lunch. But to let you know... Adam's here."

"Show him in." She turns to leave. "And Jacinta... please stay." She nods and walks out and returns a moment later, with Adam standing next to her.

"I didn't think I would see you so soon." I stand and shake Adam's hand.

"I figured I should come here personally to sign the papers, and I was also hoping to see Miss Leigh again."

I turn to look at Jacinta and see her smiling at Adam.

"It was a pleasure meeting you," Jacinta says very smoothly.

Adam smiles and I can tell he likes what he sees.

Before anyone can say another word, my office opens, and Rylee walks in, two children with her holding one with each hand. Winter runs straight for me, and a boy not much older than Winter runs to Jacinta and wraps his arms around her legs.

"Oh, sorry, I didn't realize you had a meeting," Rylee says and goes to call Winter back, who I have picked up and is wrapped around me like a monkey. *I love this kid so fucking much.*

"No, no meeting. Just thought I would come and meet more of the staff," Adam says, and Rylee's eyes narrow.

"Hi, Adam. I'm Rylee. Beckham's sister. So nice to meet you." Rylee offers her hand, and Adam shakes it before she turns back to me.

"Your niece?" I nod, and he smiles. "It's what I'm after, a family business." He turns back to Rylee, then looks to Jacinta, who's kneeling down whispering to who I guess is her son. "If you send me the papers, I will sign them immediately. Looking forward to working with you all." Adam strides out, and Jacinta doesn't even lookup.

Rylee steps over. "A kid pushed Winter over at school. Oliver saw it and pushed the kid back. He got into trouble for it," Rylee says.

I peer at Winter to see her grinning at me. "You okay?" She nods as if nothing happened and snuggles into me. When I lift my head, Jacinta is wiping tears away from her son's face as she stands and pulls him into her side.

"Do you mind if I leave early?" she asks, holding her son close to her.

"I can take him. We can go get ice cream," Rylee says with a gentle expression.

"I know you mean well, Rylee, but no," Jacinta states and then looks back at me. "Can I please take the rest of the afternoon off, sir?"

I nod, and she turns and walks straight out the door, not even looking back.

When she's gone and the door is shut, Rylee turns on me. "What did you do?" She crosses her arms over her chest.

"Oh, you in trouble now," Winter says. I put her down, but she stays right next to me.

"I did nothing. She is an employee, Rylee. Stop considering her feelings when she's at work. She doesn't come here to make friends. The woman comes here to do her job. A job I pay her well for."

"She has no one. And the one person she did have I took away," Rylee says, guilt seems to be eating away at her.

"You can't take something away that was already yours," I reply. We all know it. She even knows it. She and August, despite all the obstacles they faced, were always meant to be together. It just took them a while to realize that fact.

"Just—" Rylee starts, but I shake my head, interrupting her, "I'll go around later to make sure she's okay. Will that make you happy?"

Rylee nods and calls for Winter.

I watch as they walk out hand in hand.

"Very happy," Rylee sings as she leaves.

I scan the area. My car looks out of place parked here. It's probably worth more than every car in the entire street combined. I'm out front of a small brick home, and when I say small, I mean it. The whole structure could probably fit into the living room of my apartment. It has a tidy lawn compared to the other houses in the area. Hardly worth the maintenance if you ask me.

It took me over thirty minutes to get here. If this is how long she has to travel every day to get to work and back, I do not envy her because if she got caught in traffic, it would take twice as long.

I step up to the red door and knock. I hear the sound of a television but no voices.

No one answers, so I knock again.

The door opens, and standing in front of me is Jacinta, a pair of tanned legs topped with tiny shorts and a midriff-baring shirt encasing pert breasts. Who knew a body like that was hiding under all those clothes? I mean, I saw it when she wore that dress the other night, but it was mostly covered.

She is my employee.

And that is not something I want to mess with.

"Mr. Harley." Her voice sounds surprised. She should be. I don't make house calls often.

"Rylee was concerned," are the first words that leave my mouth, and she doesn't respond, so I continue, "How is your son?"

She wipes a hand over her face and shakes her head. "I don't understand why you're here. You don't even like me. So what's going on?" Her mouth thins to a straight line.

Sass.

Well, well, well!

Who knew she had it in her?

"Your son stuck up for my niece, so I'm here to make sure he's okay."

Jacinta's arms cross over her chest, which pushes up those pert breasts, and she breathes heavily. "Oliver is fine. He was upset, but I was able to calm him down."

"I had a friend who lived on this street," I tell her, looking away.

At the end of the street is a green house, and inside that green house is where Glenn lives. The only person who more than likely feels the same pain I do every night—my dead girlfriend's father.

I sometimes think my love for her was made up, maybe in my imagination. But when she comes to me at night, I know it was real. That I did love her.

"I didn't see you as a man who would venture over this side of town, considering you live so far away." Her mouth quirks up at her response.

"I did, very often in fact," I say, looking down the street in the direction of Glenn's home. I have good memories of that house. It was the place I used to escape the pressures of everyday life.

"Do you want to come in?" She steps back.

I look inside—it's clean, bare, but still nice.

"Did you put in the form to get your money reimbursed?" I ask, trying to keep thoughts of Paige from entering my mind.

She nods and steps back in the doorway. "I did. Thank you for that."

"I'll see you at work tomorrow." Stepping away, I go straight to my car. On the way out of the neighborhood, I drive past Glenn's house, pausing on the street out front. The lights are on, and it still looks the same. As if after all these years, time stood still right here in front of me. Unable to move forward. Incapable of advancing. Impossible to progress.

The porch light flicks on, and Glenn's figure approaches in silhouette through the glass in the front door. He won't recognize this car, so I push my foot on the accelerator to speed away. As I drive off, he opens the front door, and he looks directly at me inside the car. I know he can't see me, my car has tinted windows, but that stare feels like he can see straight through me.

That night, I try to keep those demons at bay, but sometimes demons have a way of creeping up on you.

"We can sneak out the window," Paige says as we sit on the edge of her bed.

Her father arrived home a few hours ago and walked me out, but then I snuck back in. Now Paige wants to sneak out with me.

"We can't," I reply, leaning up behind her and kissing her neck, which instantly sends shivers down her body.

"I can always say something to persuade you, so—" She likes to bribe me, and I must admit I do like her bribes.

"Let's stay in," I effectively interrupt her with a whisper, so her father won't overhear. She leans back into my touch, her body molding against mine.

"Okay then. As long as I get to keep you, I'm in." She turns and crawls up to me, pushing me back so she's hovering above me.

"You have me. Now, tomorrow, and years from now," I tell her.

A bold smile touches her lips. "Oh, this I know."

It was the second to last night I saw her alive, and that night I run over and over in my mind.

Could I have said something?

Could I have done something differently?

The answer to those questions I shall never know.

But because of that, no other woman will ever compare.

CHAPTER
6

Jacinta

The rest of the week goes smoothly, smoother than I expected, at least. Beckham still snaps at me and tells me to get lost, but he hasn't fired me this week yet, so that's a plus. When Friday rolls around, I walk into his office with all the paperwork to be signed and put it on his desk.

One good thing, we acquired the Jackpot account, and that's put Beckham in a better mood.

"Do you have plans for the weekend?"

I startle, realizing Beckham is talking to me.

When I don't answer, he raises an eyebrow, clearly becoming impatient.

"Are you talking to me?" I reply, confused.

"Yes. Does it look like I was talking to anyone else? Maybe an invisible friend of yours?" he snaps.

"I have no plans," I tell him.

"My other sister, Rhianna, is having a barbecue. Rylee asked that I invite you."

"The twin?" I ask him. They are identical, and one time I went up to the wrong twin.

"Yes, bring Oliver. Rhianna has a daughter your son's age," he says. Then his focus shifts onto the paperwork I just delivered, effectively dismissing me without further words. When I step out of the door, a police officer is standing at my desk.

"Can I help you?"

He glances past me to the door I just exited through. "Yes. I need to speak to Beckham."

The door to Beckham's office opens, and he's standing there. I watch as his eyes go wide and a vein ticks in his neck as he stares at the man in front of me.

"I saw you the other day," the policeman says, clearly looking at Beckham, who stands a little taller. "You didn't come in?"

"I didn't think I should."

"You're always welcome at my house, you know that." Beckham runs his hand over his face as he looks down. "I found a few things in her room that I thought you might want."

"You didn't clean it out?" Beckham asks as I step away from the conversation. I can still hear everything even though I'm now seated at my desk, but I thought it best to make it appear like I am not listening in.

"No, she was the only good thing in my life. To throw anything out that involved her isn't something I wish to do. Ever."

They stand there in a silent stare off for a few moments.

"You look good, Beckham. I didn't think you would follow in your father's footsteps and take over his business. Paige always said you wanted to follow your sports."

Beckham's face contorts at the mention of Paige's name. "I have work to do," he says, clearly trying to mask any emotion right now.

"Will you come around? I have a few things I want to give you."

"I'll see. Give me time. I will try to get there when I can."

The man looks around, smiles at me, and then glances back at Beckham. "August says you haven't dated since."

"August needs to shut his mouth," Beckham snaps.

"He was her brother. He cares. Even if he doesn't show it."

I knew August had lost someone when I met him, but I didn't know it was his sister. And that his sister was also the woman whom Beckham had lost.

"As I said, I'll see. Thanks for stopping by, Glenn." Beckham returns to his office and shuts the door.

Glenn turns to face me. "Sorry for interrupting your day."

I offer him a warm smile as he walks away.

Beckham stays in his office for the rest of the day.

Looking over to my right, I pull up in my car to a house that is ten times bigger than any I've ever owned or lived in. Pushing open the door, I slide out and grab Oliver, who stays by my side as we walk up to the door. Knocking only once, it swings open to reveal the spitting image of Rylee standing there. But I know it isn't her.

"I'm Rhianna." She smiles, a baby on her hip, as she greets me. "And you are Jacinta. Come in. Everyone is already here." She offers a small wave to Oliver, who waves back before he spots Winter and runs to where she's currently playing. "What's your poison? Vodka, gin, whiskey? I know it has to be something strong since you work for my brother, and he's an ass to everyone but Rylee." She waits expectantly for my answer.

"Just a water, please." Rhianna shrugs and opens the fridge. She hands me a bottle of water. A guy walks in, steps straight to her, and removes the baby from her hip. He leans down and kisses her on the lips before he turns to face me.

"I'm Noah. Nice to meet you."

"Nice to meet you as well. I'm Jacinta."

"I'm well aware of who you are. I'm glad you could come." He nods and saunters off, leaving me in the kitchen with the sister I've only ever spoken to once before, and that was because I thought she was Rylee.

"So, how's life now you can live it normally? Have you heard from Anderson or his crazy family?" Rhianna asks, pouring herself a cocktail.

"His father, Leo, got a lawyer involved, so his ex-wife, Anderson's mother, cannot contact Oliver until he's of age and can decide if he wants to know her or not. She refused at first until he offered her money."

Rhianna's eyes go wide. "She was always a

greedy woman. Whatever you two saw in Anderson, I will never know."

"I..." I go to explain why. Why I was lonely and happened to fall for a man who wasn't worthy of my time, then fell pregnant. But I don't. I don't have to explain myself to anyone.

"You two are clearly out of his league. I'm just glad he's locked away. How is Anderson's father?" Rhianna asks. "I feel like he was a silent pawn in their scheme."

I shrug. "He's sent letters, but I haven't opened them. I'm not really sure if I want to. Other than that, he hasn't contacted me."

Rhianna lifts her glass of vodka and drinks it all before she smiles at me. "You sure you don't want to get drunk with me?" She winks.

I laugh and can already tell the difference between the twins, Rhianna has a carefree attitude about her, while Rylee is more reserved.

"No, I'm good. But thank you."

"That's all right, you can watch me be a hot mess instead. It's always so much fun, especially when I get horny and Noah tries to push everyone out without being rude and puts the kids to bed." I laugh at her openness just as the door opens to the backyard, where I can see Oliver playing with two little girls, one of them August and Rylee's daughter, Winter, and the other must be Rhianna's daughter.

"That's Summer. She may or may not be annoying like me." We laugh when we see Summer put her hands on her hips and poke her tongue out at Oliver, who just looks down at the ground.

Rylee walks in, her smile bright when she sees me. "You made it. I'm so glad he passed along the message. I would have come to invite you myself, but we have some news. Good news, actually." Rylee steps over to Rhianna and reaches for her hand and pulls her toward the door, looking back at me. "Come, Jacinta, you're part of our family now, too. Come out." I know she is being nice, but I haven't been a part of a family for a long time. August was my family, and now he is hers.

I follow her outside, and when I do, I see there are more people here than I thought. I spot August, who stands when he sees Rylee and pulls her to him as she drops her sister's hand.

"What news?" I watch as Rylee looks up at August, her eyes fluttering and a smile on her face that would be impossible to break.

"August asked me to marry him."

August turns her hand around as Rylee shows the ring to everyone. I watch as her family stands and wraps her in hugs.

All except one.

"Hi, Beckham," I say, not realizing he's sitting right next to me.

He tips his head up to me and lifts his drink to say hello, then looks away.

I watch as everyone congratulates them. When they're done, one of the ladies comes over and smacks Beckham's crossed leg, and he drops it.

"Sorry, Mother," he mutters.

His mother offers me a smile, but I can see she is assessing me. "Do you plan to introduce me?" she asks.

Beckham looks to me, then back to his mother in some sort of under-no-circumstances-is-it-my-problem way.

"No. Rylee invited her. Ask her," he says with not a care in the world as he sips his drink.

"Beckham."

My head turns to the man who was in the office the other day. Today he's in casual clothes rather than a police uniform.

Beckham stands and walks off with his drink in hand to where the kids are playing. Beckham's mother offers Glenn a small hug before August steps over.

"Congrats, August. Paige would be so happy right now." I watch as pain slices across August's face, but it's gone as quickly as it appeared. "Beckham decided to walk off," Glenn says and motions in the direction of Beckham.

August then notices and introduces me to Glenn. "Glenn, this is Jacinta."

Glenn smiles. "August has told me a lot about you. It's nice to finally meet you, officially." I blush and thank him.

"It's so good to see you here, Glenn. I was hoping you would come," Rylee says as she joins us. I look at the ring on her hand and smile. It has a small diamond in the middle, which is surrounded by more diamonds that then wrap around the entire ring. It's elegant and beautiful.

I feel a tug on my leg and see it's Winter, so I smile down at her.

"Oliver wants you to come," she says in a small voice and takes my hand. I follow after her, my hand in hers until we walk up to a treehouse. It's high but not high enough that it scares me. I climb up the first few steps until I reach the door and can squeeze inside. When I do, Oliver is crying, and Beckham is tapping his back.

"What happened?" I ask, rushing over to grab him. "What did you do?" I yell at Beckham.

"Woman, will you calm down. He kicked his toe." He shakes his head. "Why the fuck would you presume *I* did anything?"

I look down to see Oliver's toe bleeding. "Buddy, it's not that bad, just a little blood," I tell him and look back to Beckham, who's watching me now with a sour expression on his face. "Why are you in a kids' treehouse?" I ask.

"Why are you?" he bites back. "I was here first." I can't help the smile that forms on my lips at his words. Winter calls for Oliver, and he scoots to the door and climbs down. His tears vanished and his pain all gone.

"You should probably leave now." Beckham pulls out a bottle that I didn't see and puts it to his lips. When he sees me still sitting here, he wipes at his lips, and his bad mood is obvious when he speaks again. "Do you not think it's weird that you're at your ex-husband's surprise engagement party?" he asks, then takes another sip. "Hell, the first guy you stole right out from under Rylee's feet. And the second, you didn't so much steal but marry him. And she still gives you a job and lets you come to her family gatherings."

"You are an *asshole,* you know that?"

He rears back at my words. "Oh, so she does have a backbone after all." He chuckles, lifting the bottle again to his lips.

"At least I'm not drinking to remove the thoughts of my dead girlfriend," I spit back at him and turn to leave, but he moves quickly and grabs my wrist.

"Keep your mouth shut about things that don't concern you," he says through gritted teeth.

I pull my arm free and sneer right in his face. "Fuck you, Beckham." With quick feet, I climb down, and when I reach the bottom, his mother is waiting.

She checks me over, then looks up the tree but says nothing.

I walk past her and hope to God I can leave soon.

CHAPTER 7

Beckham

Sitting in a kids' treehouse was not how I wanted to spend my day, but it's how I plan for the rest of this party to go.

"Beckham Harley." I groan when I hear my mother's voice. "Get your ass down here... *now*."

I could ignore her.

She may go away.

But the possibility is low.

Very low.

Because she's a powerhouse, and my mother doesn't walk away from much, even when it's best she does.

I crawl to the opening, and there she is, looking up at me.

Rylee had a tough time with mother. She wanted nothing more than for her to be with Anderson, but she wasn't aware of what a complete asshole he was to her. I almost hated my mother for that.

Almost.

"What?" I say, glaring down.

Mom taps her foot and locks eyes with me. I take a deep breath and pull myself down until I'm standing in front of her.

"He came to see you, you know." I take a step, but then the raised voice halts my stride. "Stop walking away. You've done it for too many years, and now it's time to face your demons."

"What would you know about demons?" I ask.

"I lost my first love, too, Beckham. Your father wasn't the only man I have been with. I know loss, better than the next person. And I am telling you, you need to *grow up.*"

I'm surprised by her words. Not once has she shared that information with any of us before.

"I am grown up. Just ask any one of my lady friends," I say and wiggle my eyebrows. She leans forward and clips me on the back of my head. "Ouch, what was that for?" I ask, rubbing my head over zealously.

"Go over and congratulate your sister, and for God's sake, act normal."

"I already knew... before all of you," I reply. I don't know why she thinks otherwise, Rylee and I are close.

"Of course, you did. You two are crazy inseparable. Anyone would think I had triplets," she says as she walks off. Knowing I have to follow, I do.

"Where did you go?" Rylee asks, walking up to me with a glass of wine in her hand.

"He snuck up to the treehouse," our mother chimes in.

Rylee laughs and shakes her head.

We wait until Mom wanders off before Rylee grabs the bottle in my hand and looks up at me. "Now go and apologize to Jacinta. We all heard what you said. You were rude."

Scrunching my nose up at her, I furrow my brows. Being surrounded by women isn't all it's cracked up to be. They are bossy and overbearing most of the time.

"I'm not apologizing to my employee."

"Go," Rylee snaps.

She's small, but she can be vicious. So, I give her a nod and take a deep breath. I look around for Jacinta but don't see her anywhere. What I do see is someone who I don't think I've met before standing next to Glenn, her eyes down as she reads something on her phone.

"Beckham, you remember Tamara?" I do, but only vaguely. She was one of Paige's only friends.

She looks up at me and smiles. "It's good to see you again." Her eyes rake over me, and I know that look well.

"Tamara was coming over to bring me food, and when I told her I was coming to see you, she wanted to come." Glenn lets me know. I look to Tamara and raise my eyebrow at her.

Tamara walks over and slips her arm through mine. "It's been so long. Catch me up on all things in Beckham's world."

Tamara is my type—the type I fuck, that is.

Blonde, petite, and totally doable.

Easy pickings.

She looks up at me with doe eyes, and I know what she wants and the reason she is here.

It's not just to see me.

It is what she can get out of me.

"Care to get me a drink?" she asks, looking down at my empty bottle.

"Follow me," I reply and walk back into the house.

Her hands don't let go of me, and I don't push her away either.

"I'm amazed you remember me. I never really saw you much unless you were with Paige." I wince at her using that name. She doesn't seem to notice, too lost in her own world.

Which I plan to be lost in soon as well.

It's better than my hell.

"Do you want to go to the bathroom?" I ask. My words are direct, and I don't mince them. She nods eagerly, her hands touching my chest. Usually, I would never do this. But today, well, actually, this whole week, can go fuck itself in the ass.

I lead Tamara to one of the two bathrooms and guide her in. It's simple, just a toilet and a sink. Enough for me to bend her ass over and fuck her.

As soon as the door click shuts, she pulls at her dress, lifting it until it's removed. I watch her with hazy eyes, then she reaches for my pants, undoes them, and pulls out my cock. She strokes it and leans in, kissing my lips. I let her because it's better than the alternative.

Thinking of her...

When I've had enough of her lips, I turn my head to the side and push her down. She goes willingly, drops to her knees, and the hand that was massaging my cock keeps on doing so. Her tongue darts out, and she licks the tip before her mouth covers me, and she starts sucking. I grip her hair hard and help by fucking her mouth.

My eyes close for just a second, and when I reopen them, the door to the bathroom is slightly ajar, and standing there is Jacinta.

Her mouth completely open in shock, and disgust is written all over her face. I don't miss the cold eyes, nor do I mistake the wrinkling of her nose. Perhaps disgust was an understatement. It's more like abhorrence, even revulsion.

But why isn't she moving?

I bite my lip and grip the girl's hair harder, pushing in as deep as I can go as she makes a gagging sound.

Jacinta continues to watch.

"I can always take you next. She's just warming me up," I say, and her eyes snap up to mine, and her lips press into a thin line before she sneers at me with disdain.

"You are *truly* disgusting. And girl..." Jacinta looks down on the woman who's wiping her mouth, "... think better of yourself before going into someone's private bathroom and sucking cock." Jacinta turns and stomps away. The girl on the floor, Tamara, I think her name is, stands and pulls herself into me.

"Get dressed." I push her away and tuck my cock back into my pants and rush out of the bathroom. When I turn the corner, I find Jacinta standing in the kitchen, grabbing a bottle of water from the refrigerator.

"You got some *real* attitude," I say.

Jacinta faces me, then gives me an eye roll that I'm sure her eyes will be lost in the back of her head before she turns and walks toward the door.

"Offer still stands."

She pauses at my words then turns back to look at me. She strides over and pushes her water bottle into my chest. "Sober up! You're embarrassing yourself."

I reach out for Jacinta, not giving her the opportunity to pull back from me, then lean right into her ear, and for some reason, instead of speaking, I breathe her in. *Since when does she smell this good?*

"You enjoyed it. Every damn minute of it."

Jacinta gasps and pulls back. I expect her to slap me, but her hands are clenched at her sides. She simply shakes her head and walks away, leaving me standing there.

When Tamara finally comes out, she gives me the filthiest look before she heads toward the door.

Yeah, whatever!

Good riddance.

CHAPTER
8

Jacinta

I don't look forward to going in to work the following Monday. Not at all. And to think most of my weekend was filled with images of the faces he pulled as that woman sucked his cock.

It was pure pleasure.

Why was I thinking anything about what he did?

I don't like the man.

Yes, he's good-looking, but I do *not* like him.

Not in the least.

Arriving at work at the usual time, I walk straight into Rylee's office and shut the door.

She looks up, and I glance down to her hand, the one that bears the ring. "Congratulations again."

She smiles, but it doesn't reach her eyes. "Is this weird for you?" she asks in a soft, well-mannered voice.

"No, it's not. I mean... I knew it was inevitable. We were just living, not really breathing. I want to breathe," I tell her, hoping she understands my answer. "I actually came in so I could speak to you about something work-related, if that's okay?"

She shuts her laptop and turns to me to give me her full attention. "What can I help you with?"

I look down to my feet and then glance back at her. "I want to transfer."

Rylee's mouth forms a perfect O. She looks at me a little shocked, then nods her head. "Was the pay not high enough? I know being Beckham's assistant is hard, but that's why he pays so well, knowing what an ass he is."

No, the pay would never be an issue. It's double what I was earning before working for him. Actually, it's so good, I've been saving half of it every pay, so I can have savings.

Savings.

I've never had that before.

But my well-being has to come first.

"No, I just don't think it's working out," I reply, my hands coming together to meet in some sort of attempt to calm myself down.

"Has he done something to upset you?" Rylee asks. "Because if he has, I can kick his ass."

"It's just not going to work," I relay again. I do *not* need to tell his sister about what I saw.

"Okay, well, it won't happen right away. We will need to find a replacement for you, then you will have to train her, and we will have to move you back to your old position if it's not already filled," she says.

"That will be fine, thank you." I go to turn, but her words stop me.

"He can be an ass, I know. But he isn't that bad if you give him a chance."

I don't say anything else. Just walk out the door and to my desk. When I get there, his office door is open, and I can hear him on the phone, so I get on with my day.

I don't see him again until later that afternoon when he walks out.

"Jacinta." I look up, and he's standing in front of my desk. "You wish to be let go of this position?"

"Yes, sir."

"Why?" he asks.

Oh shit! I didn't think he would ask me directly, and I don't want to tell him.

"I think you can find someone better suited than me." I give him as honest an answer as I possibly can.

His dark eyes assess me to see if I'm telling the truth.

"I approved the request. They are looking for someone now," Beckham says, then walks off.

I go back to my work.

The rest of the day, he doesn't ask me to do a single thing.

And that's okay with me.

"Jacinta."

Goddammit! I'm ready to leave, my bag in hand, which he can clearly see since the office door is open.

"Please come in here for a second."

I huff and head to his office.

When I enter, Beckham looks up from his desk and turns to face me. "You want a different position because of what happened over the weekend. Am I correct?"

"Yes." No point in lying.

"What if I said, I will act with nothing but professionalism around you if you stay?"

"I saw your cock, sir."

"And some would think you lucky." He smirks, and when he sees I am not amused, it drops from his lips. "I see. Would you reconsider?" he asks.

I bring my purse up and clutch it tighter in my hands. "You won't treat me any differently?"

"I will treat you as a regular employee if that's what you wish. But I need someone who knows what they're doing without me having to tell them. And you are good at what you do."

"Thank you." It's the first *real* compliment he has given me.

"If I act out of line again, I will let you transfer, and you can keep the salary you currently receive," he says, surprising me.

"Thank you. Can I think about it?"

"Take your time." He turns back to his computer, effectively dismissing me.

I walk out. Once I get far enough away from his door, I let out a long sigh. What the hell was that? I scratch my head, and I am sure the face I am pulling is showing my confusion.

Once I slide into my car, I finally take a deep centering breath.

I don't know if I should stay, but the pay will help Oliver and me greatly.

After I pick up Oliver, I head home. Turning onto our street, there is a car parked out the front of my house that looks incredibly out of place in this neighborhood.

"Mommy." Oliver smiles and points at the car. Red is his favorite color right now, thanks to Optimus Prime. He is obsessed. "Do you think it transforms as well?"

"No, buddy. Stay in the car while Mommy gets out. Okay?" He nods, and I pass him my phone with a game I have pulled up on the screen. When I get out, the driver's door of the other car opens, and I'm taken aback to see Anderson's father standing there.

When I walk over, a small smile touches his face.

"Jacinta, it's good to see you."

"I can't say the same. Why are you here, Leo?" My words are short and curt, and if they cause hurt, I am all for it.

"You haven't been cashing any of my checks." He quickly eyes the house then focuses back on me. "I send you enough to live comfortably. You wouldn't have to work if you chose not to."

Well, I didn't know that. Probably because I chose to never open even one of his letters.

"I did ask if you would let me know if I could meet him. If that would be okay with you."

Anderson's father looks a lot like him. He is incredibly good-looking for his age. Well-groomed and dressed in a sharp business suit, crisp white shirt, with a tie that appears like it has been tied by an expert, the knot is so perfectly executed.

But as I have discovered, looks are deceiving.

Especially for those with money.

"Leo, I don't know if I'm comfortable with that, after everything—" He holds up his hands.

"I get it. I do. And I have tried everything in my power to rectify this situation as best I can. I know I was late. I know I should have helped sooner. But I was blind to it, and I apologize for that fact. I will go... but if you could please think about it and let me know, I would appreciate it." He turns and walks to his car.

"Oliver would love to see your car, if you would allow him that?" I ask. My heart thaws a little, and Leo's face brightens, and it's the first time I have ever seen him smile like this.

"Of course, would you like me to walk away?" I look back at my car and see Oliver who's staring in awe at Leo's car.

"No, it's fine, you can meet him. Just, please, don't mention Anderson."

"I won't. You have my word."

With more than a few nerves, I step over and get Oliver out of his seat, then lead him toward Leo.

"Hey, little dude, would you like to see inside?" Leo asks, offering a friendly smile.

Oliver looks up at me for permission, and I nod my approval.

I watch as Oliver jumps in excitedly, steps all over the interior, to which I cringe, but Leo doesn't seem to care at all. He simply watches him and answers when needed.

"You can tell him to stop climbing around if you want. Otherwise, he won't stop," I say.

Leo's attention falls to me, he presses a button on his keys, and the car starts. Oliver grins and laughs as the music begins to play.

"He's fine. He seems like a good kid."

"He's the best," I say, smiling. "And smart. So far, he's excelling in his reading and already writes his name."

Leo smiles proudly. He looks back to Oliver, then speaks, "Look, I was wondering if I could speak to you... once he's done."

"Oliver needs to bathe and get ready for the night anyway. You can come in and have a coffee if you want?" I walk to the car and call Oliver out. He comes without argument, and we head toward the door. Unlocking it and turning on the lights, I tell Oliver to go have a shower. He runs off to get himself ready as I walk to the kitchen with Leo following close behind me.

"I'm just going to say it..." he pauses. "Anderson gets out on good behavior soon. I don't have an exact date, but I found out today and thought I should tell you."

"Mom, I can't find my towel." Oliver runs up behind me, and my hand falls to my heart as I turn around and smile at my son, who does look a lot like his father.

"It's on your bed where you left it," I tell him, and he nods and runs off.

When I turn back around, Leo is seated at the table, his hands folded in front of him.

"He also asked me about Oliver. I haven't said anything regarding him."

"Thank you," I say, flustered.

I open the fridge.

Then shut it.

What was I even going in there for?

"I'm going to go," Leo says, standing. "I'm sorry for bringing this bad news to you, but you needed to know." He heads to the front door and I follow him, walking him out. "If you open up any one of those letters, my number is on every single one. If you need anything, babysitter, money, new car—" I cut him off.

"Car?" I ask.

"Seems he loves mine. Would you like it?"

"Are you seriously offering me your car?" I ask in disbelief.

"Yes," he replies without hesitation.

Does he not understand that is *not* normal? People do *not* go around offering cars that are worth more than the house I'm living in.

"No. No, thank you. Ours gets us from A to B. It will do us just fine."

"Jacinta, you've done everything by yourself. Not once have you accepted money from us..." he pauses, "... but you should. He may be a shit person, but he *is* Oliver's father, and I am his father. Let me help when you need help... that's all I ask."

All I can do is nod at his words.

He leaves with no more words spoken.

CHAPTER
9

Beckham

I keep to my word. The only time I speak with Jacinta is when it has to do with work.

She stays.

I knew she would.

The money I pay my assistant is better than the highest-paid assistant anywhere else. But I also do this because I know I am an ass to work for. And the money keeps them around a little longer.

The world spins on money. I should know, it's my job.

"Are you prepared for your week?" I ask on the way back into my office, stopping at Jacinta's desk before I go into mine.

She lifts her head and bites her lip. "Yes, I think so."

Every year, Rylee and I go away to a conference and dazzle our biggest clients. It's a thank you, and this year Rylee isn't able to attend, so Jacinta is filling in for her.

"Either you are, or you aren't," I bite back.

"I am. Tickets are printed. The car will pick you up at six."

"Get the car to collect you first," I tell her and walk off to my office. When I enter, Rylee is sitting in my chair, swinging around on it like it's her favorite damn toy. "Get out," I say, but she continues to swing around again, then she flips me off.

"Why do you have such a great seat? Get me one, too," she says, not moving from my chair.

"It's late, and I have to finish a few emails before I leave. So get the fuck out of my seat."

"How about... no." She smiles. "Now, make sure you order me one."

"If I say I will order you one, will you get out of my seat?"

"If you pinkie promise," she teases.

"Fucking hell, Rylee, dealing with a five-year-old is easier than dealing with you," I spit.

She pokes her tongue out and stands. "You better order me one, asshole."

I stride around my desk and sit before she decides to annoy me further by stealing my chair again. "Why are you here?" I start my computer.

"I came to warn you."

My head spins in her direction. "Warn me?"

Rylee leans over my desk, so her eyes are at the same level as mine as she stares at me. "If you fuck this up by being an asshole, I will kick you where I know it will hurt the most."

She straightens and smiles.

So sweet, yet so sour.

Without giving me a backward glance, she saunters off out the door.

The driver pulls up to my apartment building, and I am already out front, suitcase on the ground, as the back door opens and Jacinta steps out, dressed in more casual attire than her regular work outfits.

"Good afternoon, sir. You ready?"

"I am." I climb in as the driver grabs my suitcase.

When we're seated and the car finally starts for the airport, we settle into a nice silence.

"Adam and James will be attending, and I want you to wine and dine them when necessary." Jacinta nods. "They are our biggest clients. So, *nothing* can go wrong with them."

"Got it."

"Also, villas... I will make sure yours is close to mine, so if I need to reach you, you're close by. And James and Adam will also be near ours."

"Sounds good," she says, writing away in her notebook.

"And how are you going to handle this trip? Are you fully organized with your son?"

She pauses writing and places her pen in the notebook and shuts it. When she turns to me, her hazel eyes are warm. "Yes, thank you. He is well looked after by your sister and August. Oliver is familiar with August, and he loves Winter and Rylee, so I am lucky, as I have no family."

I nod.

Not too much later, the car comes to a stop at the airport. We grab our suitcases and check-in. I purchased both business class tickets, as the flight is just over an hour to the island we are heading to.

"You didn't have to. I'm more than happy to not fly business."

"Everyone who's coming is flying business," I reply as I step along the jet bridge to the aircraft. She takes a seat next to me, and the flight attendant serves us a glass of champagne.

"I've never been on a plane," she whispers after a few moments of silence, and the plane takes off.

"What?" I say, surprised. "How is that even possible?"

"I've never left Australia. And I only left the city when I moved away five years ago, but even then, I drove."

I look away, raise my eyebrows, shocked at her words.

Looking back, I ask, "Are you scared?" Lifting my glass of champagne, I drink it all in one go.

"No, excited." And her eyes show it, they are twinkling with nervous energy, but she is animated as well, showing her enthusiasm.

"You should be. This is one of the nicest islands in Australia. It's absolutely beautiful and not overly crowded."

After we land, we deplane and board a boat

that will take us on the last leg of our trip to the island. The boat also serves more champagne and cheese platers.

"This is so..." her eyes are round with excitement, "...so posh, and probably something I would never have had the opportunity to experience." She turns to me. "Thank you for letting me come." Her voice is genuine, and I have to wipe my hands on my pants at her words because, for some reason, they have become sweaty. What's with that?

"This is a work trip. Just remember that."

She nods and looks out at the Great Barrier Reef. Her eyes take everything in as we head toward our final destination.

When the boat arrives, I watch her. It's fascinating to see something through someone else's eyes. I've been here so many times that I'm used to all the glitz, glamor, and opulence.

"Beckham, Jacinta."

We turn, after we pick up the keys to our villas, to see Adam and James. They each have a cocktail and a smile on their faces.

"Seems you got here safely," I say.

Adam offers the other cocktail in his hand to Jacinta, who takes the exotic-looking drink eagerly and thanks him.

"I'm afraid what all this drinking could do to

me." She giggles and sips the colorful liquid after she takes a few bites of the cherry on top.

"Meet us down at the pool bar after you're settled?" They both address Jacinta, and she eagerly nods her head while still holding the cocktail in her hand.

When we get to our villas, which are right next to each other, she looks over to me.

"I'm right to go to the pool bar?" she asks.

"Yes, enjoy yourself." I walk in and shut the door quietly behind me. The villa is exquisite, one of the best five-star hotels I have ever been to.

I requested villas with pool access, so from both of our villas, you can walk straight out into the large resort pool area and swim up to the bar. The bedroom has a large king bed with four posts. The colors are natural, but the room is anything but plain. The living area has a couch in the corner, and there is a large flat-screen television hanging on the wall. As I continue to check out the villa, I step into the bathroom, which includes a bathtub that could easily fit two people and a shower with two showerheads.

Walking back to the bedroom, situated on the beds in every villa, I have organized a welcome basket. I use the same company every year, and now I don't even bother asking what they will put in them because I know they are that good.

Looking over at mine it says...

Welcome, boss.

There's a small bottle of vodka, a voucher to the five-star spa, robe, slippers, eye mask. All custom-made. All personalized with the guest's name on them.

Changing out of my work clothes, I ring and order a drink to be sent to my room while I step out onto the balcony that has access to the pool and take a seat on the lounger.

"Are you sure it's okay?" I turn to see Jacinta standing there, her robe wrapped around her and a hesitant smile on her face. "That basket is amazing, by the way. Loved it."

"Is what okay?"

She motions over to some of our clients.

"You said to mingle and make them happy, but is it okay that I drink with them? Is that professional?"

"Yes. Go."

She nods, but pauses. "Do you plan to come?"

"Later. I have some calls to make first."

"Anything you need me to do?" she asks, ever so helpful.

"No."

She nods, drops her robe, and beneath it is a bright yellow one-piece swimsuit.

Her ass, round and perfect, is almost on full display as the back of her swimsuit only covers half her skin.

Fuck.

She's beautiful.

More than beautiful.

And I have to remember...

... do not fuck my employee.

That would be an incredibly bad mistake.

My cock stirs as Jacinta dives into the water. I watch her, unable to take my eyes off her as she swims over to a group of our clients. But then she turns back, and there's a wide smile on her face.

"It could be a cracker of a time if you just tried." I freeze at her words. And then somehow, somehow, I'm back to six and a half years ago, with a woman who stole me in more than one way.

How could someone be so beautiful?

"It could be a cracker of a time if you just tried." She was attempting to convince me to go into the abandoned house. I was not keen on

stepping inside that place at all. I had heard the stories, but wherever she went, I seemed to follow.

Our relationship started with friendship first, then somewhere along the way, I realized I saw her as more than that. When I told her, when I first kissed her, she laughed in my face and told me she was glad I could finally see what she had seen all along.

That we were perfect for each other.

"Not happening. Let's go back to the car." I turned back, but her hand laced itself in mine, and she pulled gently enough that I turned to look at her. Her smile could light up the sky. It sure as fuck lit up mine.

"If you make it inside, I'll let you touch my boobs."

I look down at said boobs. "I've touched and tasted them before."

She shrugged. "So you know what a prize they are then," she sung, pulling me with her, and I went because I was a teenager and the thought of touching any part of her made my cock incredibly hard. She used that to her advantage. If her father knew what we were doing, he would probably have killed us. But that never stopped Paige. Not in the slightest.

The front door was old and broken, she pushed it a little wider so we both fitted *through, and the minute we were inside, she dropped her hand from mine and started stepping back.*

"I did tell you... you could touch." The dress she wore fell to the floor. Paige was shy unless it came to me. With me, she was anything but.

Maybe it's because she realized how much I idolized her, treasured the ground she walked on.

"I would prefer it if you touch somewhere else as well." I almost forgot where we were.

"Someone could see us."

"Isn't that where all the fun is." A sinister smile touched her lips.

"I think... I love you."

I expect her to say it in return, but she always surprised me with her words.

"I know that, you fool. You just had to catch up."

And I did. I caught up.

Until ...

Until I could no longer breathe.

Until she was taken.

My sweet Paige, who was anything but sweet.

I would give this all up for her to be back in my arms.

CHAPTER
10

Jacinta

I almost forgot what a cheap drunk I am. When they hand me my third cocktail, I have to ask for a glass of water. Turns out, everyone here can drink way more than me and still be sober.

"You came to mingle."

I spin around to see who Adam is talking to. Beckham is shirtless and making his way toward me.

"I came to make sure none of you are a bad influence on my employee," he jokes.

They all laugh.

When his dark eyes land on me, he glances at the cocktail in my hand and swims over. "How are you feeling?"

"I just ordered some water."

"Oh, let her be," James's wife says, pulling on me.

Hannah, I think her name is. She's nice. Friendly. And very drunk.

This is mostly a man's trip, with only two other wives.

"We're here to have fun, after all." Hannah pushes a cocktail toward me, and I take it, holding it awkwardly as I don't plan to drink it. Thankfully, Beckham takes it from my hands.

"Thank you," I say in a hushed voice, hoping Hannah doesn't hear me.

"Are you enjoying yourself?" he asks while standing in the water next to me.

I have to remember not to look down. His chest, from what I can see, is tanned and toned. Did I expect any less from him, though?

Why are all the amazing, good-looking men assholes?

Because that's what he is.

A complete asshole.

"Yes, but I need some food," I say, realizing how late it's getting.

"Food will be sent to your villa."

I smile at his words. Hopefully, I can eat and pass out and start a new day tomorrow. Maybe with fewer cocktails. I sip the water, and when I'm finished, I can feel his stare on me. So when I look up, it's confirmed.

"Thank you." I swim off after saying goodnight to everyone.

When I walk back into my villa, I call Oliver, and Rylee answers, "Tell me he isn't being an ass," are her first words.

"No, he isn't. I swear." She sighs in relief before I hear August. "Tell her to call back later, we're building."

"I heard," I say, smiling. Oliver would be so happy right now. He loved helping August around the old house we stayed in. "Thanks again for all of this."

"It's no issue. We keep telling you this, yet you keep thanking us," Rylee says.

"I know." I chew on my bottom lip. "Anderson's father came around before I left to meet Oliver. He offered to help as well."

"And how did that make you feel?" Rylee is probably the only person I can truly speak to about Anderson with no judgment because she's been there.

"I felt he was sincere, but I just don't know."

"From what I gather, I think he is. He helped you get full rights and even kept that awful woman at bay. Maybe he sees the error of his ways."

"Maybe," I say more to myself.

"Oh, I forgot to tell you, Shandy is arriving tomorrow."

"That will be nice."

"Yes, one of her clients is out there, and they had an extra villa booked. So, I gave it to her. My brother may not be aware yet." She laughs.

"Right. So, that's going to be fun." I giggle.

"Oh, you have no idea. She loves to annoy him. It's her favorite hobby."

The next morning there's a knock on my door, and when I open it, an extremely blonde, almost white-haired, pretty woman is standing there with a suitcase.

"Shandy." I smile.

"My villa is being prepared. Can I come in?" I pull the door open for her, and she looks around.

"Well, shit! You got yourself one of the good villas. Though, from what I hear, all are amazing. But yours has pool access." She steps out, and I hear her laugh. "And your neighbor is your boss." She pauses, looks over her shoulder to me, winks, then turns back to who I am guessing is Beckham. "Good morning, Beckham."

"What the fuck are you doing here?"

"I've come to play with you. Aren't you excited?"

"No," he answers curtly.

She flicks her hair over her shoulder and steps through until she's on his balcony. I follow and see her reaching for his food.

"How come you get all the good stuff?"

Beckham's wearing sunglasses, but I know his eyes are narrowed on her.

"Because I pay for it."

"Why do you sound like that, '*because I pay for it,*'" she mimics him. Her eyes find mine, and she smirks. "Want to join us for breakfast?"

Both sets of eyes are now focused on me.

"No, I have to get ready for today."

"Are you sure?" Shandy asks with an expression I don't recognize on her face.

"I am. Are you coming to the beach with us to do activities?" I ask them both.

Shandy places her hand on the back of Beckham's chair and looks down at him. "What do you think, lover boy? Should we?"

"You should, for sure," he bites out. "Leave me the fuck alone."

Shandy looks up at me, her hand touches

Beckham's shoulder, and she digs her nails in slightly. "Loverboy here and I may do our own thing today. So you go and have some fun."

Beckham doesn't even move her hand.

Rylee did tell me they're friends.

Weird ones, maybe?

I return to my villa to dress and then run down to the beach. Everyone is already there when I arrive and have their kayaks. I take one and spend the day doing water sports. Hannah is my partner for most of the day, and when we start to get hungry, we leave them all to eat.

"So, any kids?" she asks as the waiter brings us a drink. It's my first one for the day, and hopefully, the first of not too many.

"Yes, one boy. You?"

She smiles. "No, seems that wasn't in the cards for us. Though we did try. We are actually in the middle of trying to adopt." Hannah tells me all about her and James and how they have been together for almost twenty years. I smile as I listen to her and wonder if one day I will ever get to be that lucky.

My luck with men hasn't been that good.

Apart from August—but August was different—who I guess was never really mine, to begin with. He was more my savior. Even when we were everyone's worst nightmare.

Just as we finish our food, Shandy walks out in a dress that looks incredible on her. It's a slip, and beneath that she's wearing her swimmers.

"Girls' day?" she asks as she reaches us. "I need to get so drunk that one of you two need to carry me to my villa after." She pins us both with a stare. "You get me?"

"I see you escaped the clutches of Beckham," I joke.

"Oh no, he kicked me out of his villa by pulling his cock out." She shivers. "Asshole. He knows I prefer something sweeter," she says with a sinister smile.

"Oh, God. You really saw that? And you didn't... I mean, want to just ride it?" Hannah says, and we both look at her. "What? You cannot deny that man is as good-looking as they come. We all have eyes," she says, smirking. "I may be ten years his senior, but damn—"

"Sorry to disappoint you, but no. Dick scares me. It's why I prefer pussy." Hannah almost coughs out her drink.

"What are you all discussing?" A dark voice comes from behind us.

"Your cock," Shandy says, smirking. "How ugly it is, for one."

I know for a fact it's not, but I don't chime in, even when his eyes fall to me.

"I've heard different," he says, looking away

from me and back to Shandy. "Now, did you come here to work or talk about my cock?" Beckham asks.

"I for sure don't want to talk about that, so stop getting it out in front of me."

"It's the only sure-fire move I have to get you to leave. I'll never stop pulling it out with you around if I know it can make you run. Though I must say, you are the first woman I know to run from it..." he pauses, as if he's thinking on it, then looks to me, "or second."

Hannah coughs again. "This is all too much for me. Are we drinking or planning to talk about cock all day? Because if we do, I may need to go and rub up on my husband before we continue..." This time, it's me who almost chokes. Hannah shrugs. "A woman has needs."

"That you do," Shandy says, tapping her shoulder. She turns to Beckham. "The afternoon is a boys' day, so go and play with the boys," Shandy says to Beckham.

"Who invited you anyway?" he asks, then looks at me. "We need to go over a few things later. Meet me on the balcony in a few hours." I nod as he walks away, and we all stare as he goes.

"How can you not be attracted to that?" Hannah asks Shandy, who just smiles and shrugs, sitting down next to us and ordering herself a cocktail.

"I'm immune to all that, even if I do appreciate it. I know beneath that hard exterior is a good man." She shrugs. "It's why I annoy him any chance I can get."

I laugh at her words.

She turns to face me. "He's nice to you. He isn't nice to any of his employees. That includes me, and I'm his friend."

"Oh no, he *is* an asshole." I am nodding like my head will drop off my shoulders. "I quit, but he persuaded me to stay," I reveal, to which she raises a brow.

"Money," Shandy says.

"And that if he steps out of line..." I say, finishing it there.

"Out of line? Don't tell me you've seen his dick, too?" she jokes, but my cheeks go red at her words.

"Oh, my God, you have," Hannah says, throwing her head back and laughing.

"Tell me you were *not* stupid enough to sleep with that man?" Shandy asks.

"Gosh, no. No way."

"Phew, crisis averted. Now, should we go and get shitfaced? Beckham can entertain everyone. Let's go to your villa. It's so much nicer."

This could be bad.

Very bad.

CHAPTER
11

Beckham

I hear a splash and women's laughter, and I get my answer as to where they are. Walking out to the balcony, I spot them, drinks in hand. Shandy notices my approach, but Jacinta continues to float, having no idea I'm standing here.

"Loverboy," Shandy sings, and Jacinta falls under the water, her head coming up for air reasonably quickly.

"Did you all have a good day?" I ask, my eyes locking on to hazel ones. She pushes herself out of the water and sits on the edge of the wooden veranda that leads to her villa.

"The best. How was your day smooching the clients?" Jacinta replies.

"You should get to bed. We have an early day tomorrow." My eyes stay on Jacinta, unmoving.

"We have no plans. Don't be a downer," Shandy says, pushing back into the water and floating easily. "Why aren't you out getting laid? Isn't that what you do?"

"I'm working," I snap and look back to Jacinta. "We leave early tomorrow."

"Early?" she asks, disappointment laced in her tone.

"Yes. Now sober up and pack your shit."

"Gosh, you *really* need to get laid," Shandy calls from the water.

Hannah, James's wife, laughs as she pulls herself out and says her goodbyes, leaving Shandy there with Jacinta and me.

"I'm sure you have somewhere else you'd rather be than here?" I bite.

I like Shandy. Despite our constant bickering, she is a good friend.

She knows how to push every fucking one of my damn buttons, though.

And for some strange reason, I let her.

"Nah, you are my favorite person to be around."

"What are you avoiding?" I ask. She goes under the water, and when I turn to face Jacinta, she offers me a sad smile. "Shandy ..." When her head comes back up, she locks her eyes on me. "She broke it off with me because I'm too opinionated. Can you believe that?" Shandy looks up to the sky and shakes her head. "Too fucking opinionated. Bitch, please, I'm simply too much woman for you. Your loss," she shouts to the sky.

"Come on, Shandy, want to stay with me tonight?" Jacinta asks.

I look at her and raise an eyebrow. She shrugs and holds out her hand for Shandy to take.

When they're both out of the water, Shandy turns to me. "I'm staying with you." She steps up onto my balcony and walks straight into my villa. I watch her as she heads for the bathroom, and on the way, she starts stripping, with not a care in the world. When I turn back around to look at Jacinta, I find her watching me. Her eyes are glossy with the amount of alcohol she has consumed.

"We're really going tomorrow?"

"Yes," I answer, my cock twitching in my pants at the sight of this woman in front of me.

"Okay." Her eyes lock on mine.

Quickly, I move until I'm standing in front of her. My hand touches under her chin, just skimming along her skin. "Why do you look so sad?" I ask, and she blinks. Those eyes on mine, and those lips. She has the most beautiful lips, full and luscious. They're so fucking nice that I have to force myself not to lean forward and kiss them. Touch them.

Remember...

...she is my employee.

It's not something we should be doing.

This is the reason we're leaving early.

I need to get laid.

And here, I can't do that.

"I'm not sad." For some unknown reason, she steps forward. Her body almost coming into contact with mine. "I've had a great few days, so thank you for that."

My head is screaming at me to move away.

But I have never listened to reason when I can sin instead because that's so much more fun.

"Have you?" My voice is darker, huskier than before.

She purses her lips and bites one. "Have I what?"

"Have you really had a great few days? I can think of a way to make them even better."

I expect her to push me away, to look away, but she does neither. She remains close and holds my gaze.

"Can you?" And there it is, the temptation, handed to me on a silver platter.

It's dangerous to do that.

Exceedingly dangerous.

But like any good shark, I'm going to take the bite and sink my teeth right in.

"I can." It takes two heavy breaths until my hand slides around the back of her neck. It would take one more breath for her to pull away and tell me no. But she doesn't.

I pull her to me, and she comes willingly. My lips touch hers softly and caress them. I lick her lips, tasting her, and she shivers beneath me. I can feel it go all the way through her body because ours are touching in almost every way.

And not just her shiver.

I feel everything.

The warmth that comes off her to the way her cold, wet nipples are hardening against my bare chest.

Her swimsuit doesn't leave much to the imagination, and for that, I am grateful.

"Beckham..." The word leaves her mouth, but she doesn't open her eyes as I continue to kiss and taste her.

My favorite taste. My preferred thing to eat before her would have been a brownie that was cooked just right and melts in your mouth. But I think I like the taste of Jacinta just a little bit more.

She opens her mouth for me, and I have to remember to breathe and not just inhale her smell.

When our lips connect, it's soft, gentle, and smooth.

I haven't felt this type of tremble inside me for a long time.

Pulling back, I shake my head.

When I fuck, it helps numb the pain, not bring out new emotions I have no desire to experience.

So what the fuck is going on?

And why, as I stare at her, does she make me feel anything but hate for her?

CHAPTER
12

Jacinta

I may have had too much to drink, and I may not be thinking clearly, but I can't seem to stop what's happening. My body wants what he can give me, even when he pulls away.

I didn't expect him to, but I'm not sure I can stop him either. My hand reaches out and touches his bare chest. He's smooth, with a smattering of hair in the middle of his chest and his happy trail, which my hands seem to be heading for.

He watches me, his eyes half-closed, his lashes fanning his cheek.

This could end badly.

Exceedingly badly.

I set boundaries with him, and here I am about to break them.

I wonder if I should speak, tell him about all the thoughts running through my mind, but before I can, his mouth closes in on me, and my hands dip below his loose shorts to reach for his cock. I grasp it, and my mouth opens in a gasp. This gives him access, and his tongue is quick to slide inside my mouth while his hand finds my breast and squeezes. It's rough, but I like it. A lot.

My hand squeezes his cock in return, and I wonder what it would be like to have it slide between my legs and straight in. Would it make me as crazy for his touch as I am right now?

When I breathe, I'm basically gasping for air.

The night sky is the only light out here, apart from the pool a few feet away from us. His hand leaves my breast and joins the other to slide around to my ass and lift me up effortlessly. No man has picked me up with this type of need before. I've had two lovers. One of them I fell pregnant too, and the other loved someone else.

And now, Beckham is about to make a third.

Hopefully, he doesn't love someone else or make me pregnant.

Both could be bad. Even worse than the situation at hand right now.

And believe me, there is a situation because somehow, he has gotten my top undone and falling away from my neck, revealing my breast. He lays me back on my bed, not letting go of me as he follows me down.

Our lips break apart, and as they do, he pulls his cock free and leans back toward me. I avoid looking at him because I don't want to know what he's thinking, what is running through his mind right now.

All I want is to feel.

Physically.

And he can do that, in every aspect.

But that's what has gotten me in trouble in the past.

I like to feel.

My hands circle around his back, dragging my nails up his skin as he positions himself between my legs.

It's then my eyes find him. By then, it's too late to back out, and going by the smirk that touches his lips, he knows this.

"Beckham—" Before I can finish my words, he slides in, effectively cutting me off. My legs wrap around his waist, and my head drops back at the pure pleasure my bikini bottoms lay on the floor discarded.

It's been so long since I've felt this good, this sexy. The way his hand slides up my leg and caresses it with his touch leaves fire in his wake. And I can feel it over every inch of my skin. We are nothing but hands, heavy breaths, and lips.

My gaze catches his when he pushes in farther, gaining a steady rhythm. He holds my stare, no shame and no emotion on his face.

What am I doing?

His hand slides between us to rub my clit, giving it just the right amount of pressure, and my head tilts back, and my eyes begin to close.

"Beckham."

I almost still at Shandy's voice.

Almost.

But he doesn't stop his relentless pursuit to make me come, and I don't push him off to stop him.

I hate him.

But I want him more than anything at this moment.

I think I'm really going to regret this.

But the thought doesn't stop me either.

"Fuck off, Shandy," Beckham growls, then pushes into me harder and faster. His hand that's rubbing me picks up pace, and my hands drop to the bed and clutch it tight as the orgasm hits me.

"Oh, my God," I scream. Loudly.

Beckham leans down and places his mouth over mine to shut me up, and I know for a fact that Shandy must have heard that.

I just don't seem to care.

As I kiss him back, he flips until he's under me and I'm on top, then he grabs hold of my hips and starts moving me fast. My hips rock back and forth, back and forth, at a speed I can't help that builds and builds until I'm screaming again.

What the ever-loving fuck?

How is his cock this magical?

I collapse on top of him, my body spent and my mind blown.

He pushes my hair to the side, and I feel him kiss my shoulder before he speaks, "I always knew you would be an easy fuck."

His words don't register at first, and when they do, I sit up abruptly with him still inside of me and a smirk on his face.

Goddammit! He knew what he was doing, and I was a fool to let it happen.

And I'm afraid I would be a fool who would let it happen again. And again.

But those words, those awful words, they make my hand come up, and then I'm smacking him hard across his face before I climb off of him. I reach for a towel, anything now that I'm naked, and turn back to him sitting up on his elbows. Not even bothered I just hit him.

"You've got a lot of nerve," I bark, my hands clutching the towel to my body.

"I may, but one of my nerves that was just inside your body I know you quite enjoyed. Actually, if I remember correctly, you even called me god. How many men do you call that?" He sits up fully, swings his legs off the edge of the bed, and stands.

Completely naked.

My eyes rake over him. He has long, tanned legs that are toned. He has an eight-pack, and just below that, a cock that I already know can serve me magic on a platter.

A platter for my pussy.

"Fuck, you are a *real dick*."

He glances down at his cock and back to me with a smirk. "It is real, isn't it? And he's almost ready to go again if you think you can?"

"Nope. No fucking way. Get the fuck out." I point to the door he slithered in through, but he makes no move to leave.

"This is a change. Usually, it's me throwing the women out," he comments.

"That's because I can already see what an incredible ass you are. They're blinded by good sex," I spit back at him, hugging the towel to my body as if he hasn't already seen every inch of me.

"Hmm," is all I get in response. He's looking at my body, seemingly lost in thought.

"Leave. Now," I say, hoping he will. I'm tired, and it's not just from the great sex. It's from multiple things, including my illogical mind telling me to *make him stay, do it again,* and my logical mind saying *no fucking way.*

"So you've said. Why the rush? We have all night." He starts toward me again, and I step back.

"Beckham."

I turn to that voice.

Shandy is standing on the balcony looking in.

How long has she been out there? I don't know if I want to know the answer to that question.

Shandy doesn't seem to care that he's naked. Her arms are crossed over her chest as she stares him down. "Get back to your villa and leave her alone."

"Go to your own fucking villa, Shandy. Fuck off," he bites back.

"You should leave... right now," I plead with him while holding open the glass door that leads to where Shandy is standing.

Beckham looks shocked at my words, and I don't get why.

Does he really not recall what he said to me?

Asshole.

When I look back, I see Shandy is no longer standing there.

Beckham scoops up his shorts and pulls them on before he walks toward me. When he gets to me, he smirks. "It was *all* my pleasure."

"I didn't say thank you."

"You didn't have to. It's written all over your face." He leans down to kiss my lips, and I am in so much shock that I pull away at the last second, letting him kiss my cheek.

What in the actual fuck?

Beckham walks off, leaving me standing at my door, wondering what the hell I just did.

I can't blame it on the alcohol because I'm pretty sure I'm sober right now. Let's face it, he just fucked it all right out of me.

Locking my door, I go to the bed and throw myself on the soft comforter.

It smells of him.

I smell of him.

What did I just do?

And the real question is, would I do it again?

CHAPTER
13

Beckham

"What in the actual fuck did you just do?" Shandy says as soon as I walk into the room. She's shaking her head as she walks to my minibar and pulls out a small bottle of vodka, drinking it down in one go. "You fucked an employee, which, I might add, you said you would never do. And even worse... she works directly under you. Fuck, man, how dumb can you be?"

I sit opposite her.

Shandy hands me another small bottle, and

I drink that. "Are you going to respond?" Shandy looks directly at me. "I know you, Beckham. You may think not many people do, but I do. I know you drink most weekends so you can numb your pain, or you fuck so you can feel nothing but pleasure. You have no respect for the women you fuck. Jacinta has been through enough without you treating her like absolute shit. Plus, I'm not sure you can afford to lose her."

"I can't. She's good at her job, but—"

But what?

I liked the way she tasted.

Felt.

And I would do it again.

"You're starting to see the dilemma, right?" Shandy comments.

I turn to face her, and her eyes are glossy. She's clearly drunk.

"You should get to bed."

"I was in bed. Then I heard you two yelling, and when I came to investigate, I saw you naked and her with a towel and you told me to fuck off." She shakes her head, picks up another bottle, and drinks that too.

"Shandy."

"I wish I were more like you. Not caring. It would make my life so easy to not care about who I fucked. Or if they broke my heart. How easy would my life be then? But it's not. I care. I care that my girlfriend of a year decided to break up with me because she found someone else to love her more than she said I was able to—"

"You don't want to be like me. No one does," I interrupt, my head dropping back. "I don't even want to be like me."

"You loved Paige so much that now you can't even see the good things that are right in front of you."

"You may be right, but the one good thing in my life was killed. And there's no coming back from that. No matter how hard you try."

"There is, though. You simply haven't tried. And don't tell me you have. Fucking bitches don't qualify as damn well trying. It's only one of your coping mechanisms, so you don't have to feel."

"I felt something with her," I say more to myself but for some reason out loud.

"Jacinta?" Shandy asks.

"Yep. Haven't felt like that for a long time."

Shandy sits up straight and looks at me. "It's probably because she hates you. You're used to women who fall at your feet. She doesn't fall. She takes the glider out, and you go along for the ride." She laughs at her own bad joke.

She's right, though.

But I won't tell her that.

"Rylee is going to kill you," Shandy sings. Then, before I can stop her, she clicks a button on her phone, and my sister's voice comes through.

"I'm so sorry. Are you okay?" Rylee says through the phone regarding Shandy's broken relationship.

"Your brother is here," Shandy says to Rylee.

"How's Jacinta?" Rylee asks. "She rings many times a day to check in on Oliver. It's cute. She having fun at least?"

"Oh, *so* much fun," Shandy says, wiggling her brows at me as I reach for the phone. Shandy pulls it back and shakes her head.

"Huh?" Rylee says.

"Beckham is caring for her *every* need," Shandy says with a laugh.

"What?" Rylee says. I reach for the phone again to hang up, but Shandy pulls it away and cackles loudly. "Did you really fuck her?"

Rylee screams. "Fucking hell, Beckham, she works for you. She's a nice girl."

"It'll be fine," I say.

"Yeah, whatever. Nothing is ever fine with you."

"Go to bed. Shandy, hang up and stop causing trouble just because your own life is a shit show."

"Hey," she says as I stand and walk away, heading for the shower.

As I step in, her smell instantly falls off me. Throwing my head back, I wonder if fucking her was the smart thing to do.

But I had no choice.

My body wanted it.

It wanted her.

I may pay dearly for this.

But it was totally worth it.

CHAPTER
14

Jacinta

His mirrored sunglasses reflect my approach the next morning as we get on the boat that will take us to our plane. I saw no one this morning, and I was thankful for that. My head is sore, and I hardly slept a wink. My dreams consisted of his hands on my body, roaming around, then what they could do if I let him touch me again.

It's dangerous.

It is stupid.

We sit opposite each other, and he doesn't speak the whole trip. He works on his phone as I lean against the edge looking out over the water.

If you have never been to the Whitsundays, I highly recommend you go. The water is next-level, crystal clear, pristine, and so incredibly blue. It's the most beautiful thing I've ever seen.

When we arrive, Beckham stands and walks off without me. I take my bag and follow him straight to the plane that is waiting for us.

He doesn't speak to me on the flight home either.

I pretend to sleep, so even if he wanted to talk, I'm choosing my own path.

As soon as we land, I'm off, straight out to where I left my car for the weekend.

"I'll see you Monday." I stop at that voice behind me, and when I turn to look over my shoulder, he has his glasses covering his eyes.

"Okay," is all I manage to say.

Do we pretend what we did, didn't happen?

I'm not really sure how it works. But I am also fine with playing dumb. Because now I have to look for a new job, and while I do, I somehow have to go into work every day and see him there without showing how I feel.

Rylee is standing at my door with Oliver next to her, and they are both grinning at me. When I open it, he barrels into my legs, hugging me tight, and I pick him up and hug him back.

"I missed you."

I kiss his cheek. "I missed you more." And I did, I always will. When I put him down, he runs to his room, leaving me standing there with Rylee.

"Are you okay?" she asks.

"I'm fine," I reply, smiling. She stares at me, and I instantly know that she knows what happened. "You know?" I ask.

She nods. "I do. Do you need me to transfer you? What he did is not okay."

It wasn't only him. We both had a part in it.

"No, it's fine." I check on Oliver, who's going straight to the fridge before I look back to Rylee. "Do you want to come in?"

"I just wanted to make sure you're okay."

"I'm fine. I'll be fine," I tell her.

Her head drops to an angle. "I feel like you tell yourself that, but you don't really believe it."

"Beckham..." I don't finish my thought because when I turn around, a car I don't recognize pulls up behind Rylee's. A blond man gets out, and my heart rate picks up as I take a step back into the house, somehow hoping he never saw me.

Even though I know he did.

"What the fuck! When did he get out?" Rylee states. Her history with him is much deeper than mine, but that doesn't mean I don't have one with him as well. He is, after all, Oliver's father.

"I don't know," I manage to say.

"I wouldn't recommend coming any closer," Rylee says.

"I'm not here to see you." His eyes fall to me. He looks bigger, different, but still Anderson. I'm not even sure what I saw in him all those years ago. Maybe I had too much to drink, I'm not sure, but I was stupid. I know that much. "I came to see our son."

"You can't just turn up to her house demanding to see your son," Rylee butts in.

I grab her arm and squeeze it. She is visibly shaking, and I don't blame her, considering all the things he's done to her. How he tried to control and hurt her so badly she ended up in the hospital.

"Can you please go in and make sure Oliver stays inside?" I ask Rylee.

Her gaze bounces from him to me, then back to him. "I don't want to leave you alone with him."

"I'll be fine. Please. All I care about is Oliver."

She nods as if she understands, then walks inside, and I shut the door behind her. I step down until I'm closer but not within reach, and I glare at him.

"You can't see him," I say firmly.

He grinds his teeth. "I understand I have

issues. I've taken classes. But I am also that kid's father, so I should get to know him."

"You signed away your rights," I tell him.

"I'm contesting that… it won't hold up in court."

"You never cared about him before, so why start now?" I bite back.

Anderson shakes his head. "Because I've come to realize he's all I have. And I *will* fight for him, Jacinta. No matter how far you run, this time, I *will* fight for him."

"Maybe you should leave. This is most definitely *not* the way to go about this." I take a step back, and he looks to the house. "I know I have fucked up, but I want to be a part of his life."

"You've come to this conclusion after what… a few months in prison?" I laugh at him, but my laughter is forced. "No, it takes longer than that."

"My father sees him, does he not?"

"Maybe you should ask him that. I will not discuss your father with you."

Anderson smirks. "He's an ass and tells me to grow up and fuck off."

"Well, he's right. You have always had everything handed to you, so it's about time you tried to grow up and do things on your own."

Just as he's about to say something else, August pulls up with a screech. He jumps straight out of the car and walks to me, his hand coming in front of me to block me from Anderson as he pushes me back.

Anderson holds his hands up in surrender. "I didn't come to cause harm."

"What the fuck are you doing here?" barks August.

"I came to see my son. You should know what it's like not being able to see your child." August does, but that's because he wasn't aware he had a child because back then, he moved away and cut all contact with Rylee. Until one day, he came back, found her, and the rest is history for them.

That will not be Anderson and me.

We will not get a happily ever after.

It's not in our cards.

"Glenn lives down the road. Should I call him and tell him you're in the vicinity of Rylee when you know you aren't meant to be?" August growls.

"How the fuck was I meant to know she was here?" Anderson says to August, then looks at me. "I came to be civil and talk to you. I'll be back." He turns and heads for his car.

"You aren't welcome here, Anderson. Don't ever show up like that again."

Anderson stops with his hand on the door then turns back to me. "Do you think you can keep me away from my son, Jacinta?" The way he speaks, it's like a threat, and August touches my shoulder because he knows it as well. I watch as he starts toward Anderson, but I grab his arm and pull him back.

"I can. It's my right as a mother to protect him from those who would cause him harm, and you will, Anderson. Fuck, you absolutely will. Maybe not physically, but if he turns out anything like you, that will be the same way your mother harmed you."

He doesn't say anything to me in reply, simply shakes his head, and gets in the car.

We watch him leave, and it isn't until I can no longer see his car that I feel like I can breathe again.

How does he even know where I live?

I moved and ran away from him for a reason.

I changed my name.

Started a new life.

All because his family has power.

They have the money to fight me for my son, money I could never dream of.

I was too afraid they would win to come back here, but then I had August, and we came back. And though it may not have turned out the way I had hoped, I still have Oliver, and he's my main concern. He is my everything.

"Do you want to come and stay with us?" Rylee appears, and I turn to her and try to stop the tears that leave my eyes, but I can't. They fall, and there's nothing I can do to stop the torrent.

Her arms wrap around me and hold me tight.

We are very unlikely friends. I'm not even sure how it happened, but I'm glad it did. People are drawn to her, and I am, for sure, one of those people.

"No, no, I will be fine. I'll call the police if he comes back."

Rylee pulls back and goes straight to August. "He isn't stable. You never know what he's going to do," Rylee says.

"I know, I get it. But I've lived enough of my life running from him and hiding. I don't want to do that forever."

"Okay, well... you know where we are if you need us." August kisses the top of Rylee's head, and he sniffs her. It's as if he has to embed her smell into him. It's subtle and cute, and I love how much they mean to each other.

"Thank you," I say, and I mean it.

"Now, can we talk about my brother?"

"What about Beckham?" August asks, looking between us. "Is he being an ass at work?" I avert my eyes. "Oh, okay, I get it. I'm going to head inside now."

When I look at Rylee, she's smirking.

"Do you like him?"

"No." I know she means her brother. "He's a damn asshole," I tell her.

"That he is," she agrees. "But he is also pretty amazing if he lets you in." She shrugs.

"That will *not* happen. And what happened between us will *never* happen again," I say more to myself than to her.

"Okay, that's fine. If you want to transfer, just tell me. It's got to be awkward for you, right?"

"No, not really. If he can act professional, I can, too."

Rylee raises an eyebrow. "I'm going to not comment on that. I guess we will see how it goes?"

"Yep."

"Okay, well, Shandy and I are having a girls' night out this Friday because she needs it after her break up. Would you like to come? August already said he can have Oliver if you're keen?"

I look back to the house.

"Sure."

"Good. Come over after work, and we can get all done up, feed the kids, then go out."

I nod as we walk back inside. The last time I went out with the girls, I met Anderson and fell pregnant.

Yes, that's how boring my life is.

And the time after that, I got drunk with a few girls, and I slept with my boss.

Damn, my track record for drinking doesn't look good.

CHAPTER 15

Beckham

Jacinta's at her desk when I walk in. She's sitting there in a tight dress that hugs all her curves. And believe me, under that dress are perfect curves. Curves that I traced with my hands.

I like a woman with hips.

Her hazel eyes shoot up to meet mine, and she smiles, but I don't return it.

"Good morning," she sings.

It is *not* a good morning.

This morning I woke up with a fucking hard dick that I had to pull in the shower just to get it to soften.

And that shit's all because of her.

I hate her.

But I would like to bend her over her desk and fuck her again.

The struggle is real.

"Why are you here early?" I bark.

"Because you sent me a message last night asking me," she says, the smile still on her face is driving me crazy.

"Why the fuck are you smiling?"

She shrugs, the smile not leaving. "It's a good day."

Somehow, I contain the eye roll.

"Nothing is ever good about Monday."

"We have two meetings straight away, your coffee is on your desk, and the first client should arrive at any second."

I eye her. "Bring him in when he gets here." With a quick spin, I walk into my office, and just like she said, my coffee is on my desk along with the paperwork needed for today.

Not long later, the client arrives, and Jacinta

laughs at something he says before they sit. I keep my eyes off her while she sits there and takes notes, and when we're finished, she stands and escorts him to the door with her hand on his shoulder as she giggles. Dammit! I have to remember not to call her out. To act professionally. But when she continues to walk with him, I call her back. She says goodbye, and when she returns, the smile that was on her face is still there.

"What can I do for you, sir?"

"Stop trying to fuck my clients for one?"

Her smile falls and fast. "What did you just say?" Her hand goes directly to her hip.

I get out from behind my desk and walk over to her. "Did I stutter?"

"Beckham."

We both turn at my name being called. Archie walks in, and he smiles at me, and when his eyes fall to Jacinta, I see the glint of admiration in them. He likes what he sees.

"Do you not know how to knock?" I ask.

Jacinta's eyes go wide, and she pastes a welcoming expression on her face, playing it off when Archie looks at her.

"No, not when I pay you what I do. Now, where the fuck is my money?"

"Where you left it! In the bank, in a trust account. How much have you fucking smoked today?"

"I'll just head out," Jacinta says quietly while pointing to the door.

"No need, sweetheart. I'm just here to pull his balls. Someone needs to since it seems the only people who like to give him a taste of his own medicine are his sisters. Everyone else is too scared to tell him how it is." Archie smirks.

Archie and I went to school together. Our lives took different paths, mine on the straight and narrow, Archie's not so much. Archie's mother went bankrupt after we finished school, and while I was drowning in my own pain, Archie decided to create his own business.

Boosting and selling stolen cars.

He's good at it too.

Among other things, I'm sure.

"She can leave," I snap at Jacinta, Archie doesn't get to say if she stays or not.

"Yes, yes, I will. Seems you don't need me for the rest of the day since you seem to think I have ulterior motives anyway. I'll be on my way. Have a good day, sir." Jacinta goes to leave, but I catch her before she can, my hand circling her wrist. She's angry from my earlier comment, I like it.

She pulls it back, and her eyes zoom in on me. "Don't you fucking touch me again," she says with venom coating her tongue.

"You didn't seem to complain last weekend," I reply with a smirk. "Speaking of that—" She puts her hand up in front of my face, effectively halting where I was going. "No, we shall *not* speak of that. That is the last thing I ever want to think about again. Good day, Beckham. I'll see you tomorrow when you decide to come to work with a bit less attitude." She stalks off, and I hear laughter behind me. Archie is sitting in a seat in front of my desk with a cigar to his lips and smoke drifting up like billowing clouds, one leg crossed over his knee.

"I like her," he says. "Keep that one around."

"Did you simply come here to annoy me?"

"No, I'm your next client. You would know that fact if you bothered to check your itinerary."

Shit, I forgot to check my client list.

Jacinta takes care of it, but for some reason, I didn't check the list she left on my desk this morning as meetings were one after the other. Usually, Jacinta lets me know, but I guess with everything happening, she either forgot or was so angry she didn't care.

"So, who's the hottie, and have you fucked her yet?" Archie is smiling, and his eyes are sparkling with mischief.

"Fuck off."

"Oh, so you did." He rubs his hands together. "Mixing business with pleasure. Never thought I would see the day." The laughter is deafening, and his whole body is shaking with the power he has put behind it. He is, of course, laughing at my expense.

"This is something you're familiar with?" I question, knowing full well how many personal assistants he has lost over the years due to his indiscretions. "And how does that usually work out for you?"

"Well, the last mechanic I tried to fuck, let's just say she chased me around with a wrench, and when she couldn't catch me, she threw a hammer at my head. Just missed, but the Maserati wasn't so lucky."

"Yeah, so now you understand why I take no advice from you." I sit back in my chair as he puffs on the cigar, billows of smoke wafting around my office space. "Put that damn cigar out before the alarms go off," I growl.

"Personally..." he smirks, his bottom lip tips

up as he does, "... I think you need to put out another fire, one that has nothing to do with my cigar and more to do with a hot secretary." He laughs, and I throw the nearest thing I have at hand right at his head, only this time it doesn't miss.

CHAPTER
16

Jacinta

"He isn't always an ass." I jump at the voice behind me as I stand in line at the café. "No, actually... come to think about it, he is." It's the guy from Beckham's office, his friend and client. He holds out his hand, and I'm inclined to give him mine. Not only because he's good-looking, but he scares me a little. He has that whole brooding gangster look down pat. "The name's Archie."

It isn't in the way he's dressed because he dresses well—suit, black button-down shirt, white tie, and the shiniest black shoes I have ever seen. Honestly, I could use them as a mirror to apply makeup. There's a tattoo peeking out of his collar weaving up his neck, but that's not necessarily the reason he gives off this persona. No, it's in the way he holds himself. It makes me want to look the other way, even when he smirks at me.

"Jacinta."

Archie nods and shakes my hand, gripping it softly but using force as well. I pull away and turn back in line to order my food before I need to leave to pick Oliver up from school today instead of sending him to afterschool care.

"He's about to walk in, you know, just in case you want to run," he whispers as I start to order. I look back over my shoulder and see Beckham. "He caught you, so I guess you can have lunch with us." Archie steps up next to me. "I'll pay for whatever the lady wants," he says, then proceeds to order his own. After he pays, we both step away for the next person, and I blindly walk to where Beckham is sitting. Archie pulls out my chair, and I take a seat and cross my legs as Beckham's dark eyes lock onto mine.

"Thought you had to run?"

"Play nice. I invited her," Archie says. He sits as our coffee comes out, and as they do, he takes his and stands again. "It was a pleasure meeting you, Jacinta. I'm sure we'll see each other again."

"Where the fuck are you going?" Beckham says.

Archie smiles down at me, fixes his tie, and gives Beckham a friendly glare.

"I have needs to be met, and it appears you two do as well. Enjoy." He saunters off after those parting words, and when I turn to look at Beckham, he's watching me.

"You're a real dick, you know that? You can't even keep it professional at work!" Crossing my arms over my chest, I sit back and wait for him to speak.

He says nothing, just glares at me.

"Really?" I bark, then shake my head. Standing and gathering my things, I don't even bother waiting for my food. "I'll see you tomorrow. Any more of what happened today, and I *will* quit." I walk out and feel him behind me. I don't look back, though. I keep walking until I get to my car. Using the key, I open the back door and toss my bag inside, then turn around to find him standing there. "Did you just stalk me?" I ask him incredulously. "You know that's illegal."

"Hmm," is all I get in response.

I watch as his dark eyes darken just a fraction before he reaches out and grips my hip with a strong hand. I should be stopping him, pushing him away, but I'm a slave to his touch. When he has his hands on me, I seem to forget the world even exists because all I can feel is him. Before I can push him away or even think rationally, his other hand grips my face so his palm is covering my cheek, and he leans down and kisses my lips pushing me into the back seat of the car.

I feel his body rub up against mine, feeling every inch of his hardness. I shouldn't want this or even need this.

The two of us?

We are bound not to work.

We are bound to explode.

I didn't see that with my other relationships, but for some reason, with Beckham, I do. And let me point out we are *not* in a relationship, and I don't want that. I'm enjoying being single, being me, doing what I want to do. My life is my own right now, apart from my beautiful boy, who I adore having around.

My hands reach for his sides, and I grip onto his shirt for dear life as he kisses me.

I wish he would stop kissing me.

No, I don't.

Not really.

But I do.

Beckham pushes me back and lifts one hand to cover my head as he ducks me further into my car, so my back hits the backseat, and he's hovering over the top of me. His hand sneaks between us and slides up my skirt until he reaches my panties and rubs my clit. He applies pressure, kissing down my neck, taking his time as he does. Due to our position, my hands are stuck, and I'm forced to remain clutching his shirt.

I start breathing heavily as he slides one finger under my panties and inside me while he bites my nipples through my shirt. How he knew the exact spot that turns me on, I may never know.

I hear a car, and my body freezes.

My hands clutch him, but he doesn't stop moving.

And because he doesn't, I have to try even harder to fight the orgasm from building, even though I'm afraid any second now we will get caught. Fuck, someone could be watching me get my rocks off right now.

"My body is covering every inch of you. Knock it off," he growls into my ear before he bites it.

This is so unfair.

"You are an asshole," I say, my back arching into him.

"Yes, I may be. But you are the bitch beneath me about to come." He chuckles, and I can't even argue with him about the fact he just called me a bitch. Because his hands are working faster, he's grinding into me at the same time, and my senses are going into overdrive with how much I'm feeling right now.

"Fuuuck." The word explodes from my mouth with so much emphasis, and as it does, his hands leave me and he grips my face, kissing me, shutting me up. The breath that I need to catch now is his breath. And Beckham doesn't seem to mind at all.

He takes a deep breath and then he's off me.

No more kisses.

No more hands touching me.

I try to sit up and pull my skirt down, and when I finally manage it, I see him fixing himself in his trousers before he looks down at me, turns, and walks away.

What on earth am I doing this for?

And the bigger question?

Why is he?

Beckham's already closed off in his office the next day when I arrive. I slept like a baby last night thanks to him, but I would never tell him that. Actually, ever since we had sex, I've been sleeping well. Maybe I needed to release some stress. I just didn't realize I would use my boss to do so.

We don't talk, apart from me letting him know when his appointments arrive.

And the rest of the week goes by exactly the same.

He makes no smart-ass comments. His eyes don't wander to what I'm wearing. He keeps it all to himself and remains lost in work.

It's Friday, and I'm going out tonight. Oliver is so excited to spend the night with August and Winter. I'm getting ready to leave the office for the weekend, slipping my heels back on, when I notice Beckham is standing at his door.

"Come in here for a minute and shut the door." I grab my purse and do as he says. He's standing in front of his desk, leaning on it, his legs crossed in front of him as he watches me.

"Shandy has invited Archie and me tonight."

Well, shit. I nod, but my body tenses. I can't help it.

"I've declined."

"Okay." My body instantly relaxes, and I take a deep centering breath.

"Have a good night, Jacinta. See you on Monday." He smirks, and I turn to walk to the door, more than a little confused. When I pull his office door open, I glance back at him and see his smirk hasn't dropped from his face. I offer him a small smile as I shut the door behind me with a click. Grabbing my things, I head to Shandy's work area only to find she's already left for the day.

Rylee walks out of her office, paperwork in her hand and a pen between her lips. "You leaving?" she mumbles, and I nod. "Okay, good. I should be home in the next hour or so... I just have to finish a few things. I'll see you at my place, though, right?"

I give her a nod and continue to the elevator. Pressing the button to go down, my phone dings, so I retrieve it from my bag.

Shandy: Don't hate me...

I press call, not knowing what the hell she's going on about and she answers straight away.

"Why would I hate you?" I ask, confusion causing my eyebrows to pull together tightly as I step out of the elevator and make my way to my car. Now, every time I look at the back seat, I see him there, on top of me, doing things with his hands and mouth.

Dangerous.

Risky.

Precarious.

"Well, because I invited Beckham. He's one of my best friends, but I didn't realize until after how it might affect you. So, I'm sorry."

I smile, even though she can't see me through the phone. "It's okay, he told me," I reply. "Look, I've got to go. I'm about to get Oliver and find something to wear. What are you wearing?"

"A dress. I need a new wife." She giggles. "Make sure it's short and hot. You need to find some arm candy, too," she sings into the phone.

I have a feeling tonight isn't going to be what I expect.

Hopefully, I can slip out and leave early without anyone noticing.

CHAPTER
17

Jacinta

He lied. I knew it. I should have guessed it straight away. I clutch my drink in my hand as he walks toward us, dressed more casually than usual. He's wearing black jeans with a white shirt, which would probably be casual on someone else, but not him.

"Yeah, you came." Shandy jumps into his arms. I turn away, so I can't see his eyes on me, and sip my drink. Why did I decide to drink again? Like some sort of sixth sense, I can feel when he comes up next to me, not even having to turn to know it's him.

Intuitively I just know.

It's not only his smell, but there's something about him that makes normal perception hype up and become something more.

"Jacinta." A man drops into the chair in front of me—Beckham's friend, Archie. He nods to my drink and sits back, lifting his own. "Do you dance?"

"No."

"Bullshit! She's been dancing for hours. Beckham, take her out dancing," Shandy says. When I turn to face her, it's him I come face-to-face with.

"I don't dance," Beckham says through gritted teeth, his eyes on my lips. I lick them like every cliché book I've read.

When a man is staring at your lips, and you know exactly why, why do you always seem to lick them?

Because despite me saying I don't want him, I know it's the exact opposite. I want him with every fiber of my being.

"I'll take you to dance, sweetheart," Archie says with a raised brow.

"You don't like most people. Why are you even talking to her?" Beckham asks Archie.

Archie smirks at me, and I can't help the smile I give in return.

"Don't entertain the asshole," Beckham barks at me.

"That's exactly why. Because you're interesting when you're riled up," Archie says. "Plus, she's beautiful, and I would like to see her dance. Wouldn't you?" Archie goes to stand, but Beckham does first and reaches over and pulls me up. Now on my feet, he tugs me out of the area where we're seated.

"I don't want to dance with you."

"Too fucking bad," Beckham says. When we get to the crowded dance floor, he turns and pulls me to him, so our bodies are aligned, not caring that we aren't dancing to the rhythm of the music, only that our bodies are in full contact with one another. I feel him move my hair from my shoulder before his lips connect with my skin, and his tongue licks from my shoulder to just under my ear. A shiver breaks out across my body, and I lean into him a little more, and the world around us evaporates.

Completely.

Our hips sway, my head rests on his chest, and his mouth stays on my bare shoulder, his hands resting just above my ass, gripping onto my hips.

I could pull away.

I should pull away.

But it feels too good, which seems to be the dilemma with Beckham.

And I'm afraid if I don't get the courage soon to pull away, I may never be able to.

He's not like Anderson, and he's nothing like August either.

Beckham is his own brand of man, and I'm fast falling into his trap.

"Is this why you haven't been answering my calls?"

I pull back at those words because they're clearly directed at us. And they are so close I can hear them even through the loud music pumping through the club. Beckham keeps his hands on my hips, not letting me get away.

"Who even is she?"

Now that I can actually see her, I smile, but her eyes zero in on me, clearly not happy.

"What the fuck are you looking at bitch?"

I pull away from Beckham now to see he's visibly angry.

"This is not a *me* problem," I say to Beckham and back away. "He's all yours, sweetheart." Smiling, I turn and walk back to our table, all eyes are on me and wide with surprise. Rylee is back from the bar with two drinks in her hand, and she passes one to me. Archie is sitting there messaging on his phone, then he lifts his eyes as I take a seat that's available near him.

"I see you met one of his crazies." Archie laughs. Then his face goes from smiling to serious. All playfulness leaves his expression as he focuses on me. "Beckham is probably the only person on this planet I care about. I'd literally kill someone if they hurt him again." He pauses, looks me up and down. "You feel me?"

"No. I do not. And was that a threat?" I ask with my eyebrows raised. No one will ever be threatening me again. I've had enough of that to last me a lifetime.

"Of course not, just simply informing you." Archie stands and wanders off, and Rylee sits next to me, watching Archie leave and nudging me with her shoulder. "You okay?"

I shrug. "A little drunk, but fine." I smile.

"Archie is…" she looks away as she speaks, "… let's just say he doesn't like anyone but Beckham. And, well, Beckham hardly likes anyone." She laughs. "Archie's scary, I get it. But he can see what we all see."

I squint, my brows pulling together. "Huh?"

"We see the way Beckham is around you. Even if he says the wrong things, his actions with you are different to anyone else. Archie can see it. And because he remembers what happened last time Beckham lost someone, he doesn't want that to happen again."

"Is he dangerous?" I ask, completely ignoring everything else she said. I don't want to know that she thinks her brother sees me differently, I prefer how we are now with no talk of emotions.

"Only to those he hates." She giggles. "Which is almost everyone." She shrugs.

"We should go," Beckham says, standing in front of me. Thinking he's talking to Rylee— because clearly, he isn't talking to me—I don't respond. "Jacinta." This time he says my name.

Is that the first time he's called me by my name?

Am I that drunk that I can't remember?

"What?" I crinkle my nose at him.

He offers me his hand. "It's time you got home. Come..."

"Come?" I laugh. "No, thanks. I'm good." I turn away from his hand to see Rylee holding in her laugh.

"We need to talk, and I can drive you home while we talk," he says again.

Looking up at him, I have to remember what an asshole he is. Because who says no to going home with a man who looks like him? Dark hair matched with dark eyes and a face that could stalk a runway, he has well-defined, everything.

"I'll take a hard pass. How does that sound?"

"That sounds like a no," he says, and before I can say anything else, he leans down and swoops me up. Throwing me over his shoulder, he carries me through the crush of bodies. I thump his back to let me down, but it doesn't work. I lift my head to see Rylee is waving and smiling at me as I go. He pushes through the crowd to the exit, and the cold night air hits my bare legs.

"Put me down before everyone sees I'm not wearing panties," I tell him.

He slides me down his front, one hand on my dress, being super careful to not let it ride up. "Now, where were we?" Greedy hands reach for me again, and I welcome the warmth, even when I shouldn't, as he cups my chin in his hand. "Yours or mine?"

"Who was that girl?" I ask.

"Nobody," he answers, as our eyes lock on each other. He stares, blinks, and doesn't look away.

"Who was she?"

Beckham pulls back, and my body is cold from the loss of him.

How fucking ironic.

"I told you, she's nobody."

"So, you fuck a lot of nobodies then?" I ask, hand going to my hip and jutting it out to one side. "Do you think I'm that stupid? That I don't know you're fucking her?" I ask, giggling. "You can fuck who you want, but why not just say so?"

"Because I fucked her once, and she won't leave me the fuck alone. Now, can we end this? It's getting cold, and your bed is getting colder the longer we stand here."

"You think you're real smooth..." I say, the cold air sobering me up just a little bit more.

"Well, I am." He reaches for me again and pulls me in fast so that I have to put my hands on his chest to stop myself from crashing straight into him. "It's cold. Let's go."

"You mean before I change my mind," I say, pulling back as he reaches for the keys in his pocket. He grabs hold of my hand and starts walking, and I blindly follow the lion like a lost sheep.

"That won't happen. You like the way I fuck you. Plus, tonight I plan to have dessert, then fuck you, too." He stops at his car, and I look at it, my eyes going wide. I've seen this car, know it's his car, but have never been in something so expensive in my life. My hand reaches out to touch it—I could never afford anything like this in my life. Ever.

Growing up, we didn't have a lot of money, but we weren't poor either. My parents were careful with how they spent their money, and buying something like this to them would seem a waste.

"She's a real beauty, isn't she?" he says as I lift my hand away from his car. When I turn to face him, I wonder if he was talking about the car or me because his eyes are glued to me, and I can feel the heat radiating off him. But that couldn't be possible. That would mean he was giving me a compliment, and when the hell does he ever do that.

"I guess so," I say as he pulls open the car door and I slide inside. My phone buzzes as he rounds the front of the car. It's Shandy and Rylee, both messaging me with emojis. I laugh and slide it back into my purse as he climbs in. After starting the engine, his hand goes to the gearshift, and he pulls out. I watch, fascinated. He makes driving look hot. The veins in his arms pulse and he clutches the gearshift hard.

We don't speak, and the few times he glances my way, his smirk sits on his lips. Until we get to my place. He gets straight out like he knows what I'm thinking and opens my door, offering his hand.

I shouldn't be sleeping with my boss.

Again.

But I just can't seem to say no.

Again.

Beckham follows me to my front door while I grab out the key and unlock it. The minute the door is unlocked, I feel him behind me as he pushes me in, his body at the back of mine, and he reaches for my purse, dropping it to the floor as he kicks the door shut behind him. Hands slide up my bare arms, sending goosebumps all over my skin, then slip to the middle of my back and unzip my dress so it falls and pools on the floor at my feet.

I'm naked, apart from my panties, which I might add I am wearing even though I said I wasn't because I wanted him to put me down. He has no trouble sliding a finger through the side string and pulls them down with a smirk at the realization that I do, in fact, have them on. Turning me as he does, I'm now standing in front of him, and he drops to his knees then kisses my belly button.

I'm helpless to do anything.

To stop him.

To even want to.

My mind and body haven't caught up with each other, and I don't think they intend to.

A finger slowly slides between my legs, making them shake, as his mouth drops lower and lower to between my legs. The two meet at the same time, and he slides one finger inside of me as the other hand grips my ass to pull my body even closer to him. I feel his breath between my legs, and my hands move to grip his hair to hold myself in position as he does something so dangerous.

Beckham licks me, almost making my legs give way with the sensation.

He holds me to him though, not letting me fall, as he lifts one of my legs over his shoulder.

My hands stay in his hair, gripping it as he works his tongue between my legs. The lights in my house are off, but the light from the streetlamp outside shines in so I can see the outline of him. He smacks my ass, then grips it hard with his hands as I start to shake again. He reinserts his finger and starts pumping into me, hitting that perfect spot as he fucks me with his tongue.

When I come, I fall, and I'm not even joking, as my hands let go of his hair and the one leg I was balancing on gives way, and I can no longer keep myself upright. He catches me, easing my fall as I go and lays me down. He stands, his fingers grab the bottom of his shirt, and in one swift movement, it's off over his head and dropped to the floor. He kicks his shoes off, then removes his trousers. All the while, his eyes are locked on mine.

Naked, on the floor.

It's as if he thinks I'll run away.

I couldn't even if I wanted to because my legs won't work.

The minute I see his cock, my legs clench, knowing what is about to come and what he is about to give me. And knowing full well I am going to like it.

He reaches for me, I give him my hand, and he lifts me like a rag doll, so I have to wrap my body around him. I feel him at my entrance, hard and wet, all mixed in one as I wiggle in his hold.

I want him. Even if I don't have the energy, I want him.

"Jacinta," he whispers in my ear.

I pull back to look at his eyes and see him smiling before he starts lowering me onto his hard cock.

And let me tell you, what a fucking cock it is.

Eyes so dark smile at me as I moan from the pleasure.

Then my back hits the wall, and my hands clutch his shoulders as he grips my ass and starts moving me up and down, faster and faster.

"Who's my good little whore?" he whispers.

To let him know I don't like his words, I dig my nails into his shoulders, which only makes him fuck me harder. "Tell me... tell me how much you like it when I fuck you like a whore."

MY CRUEL LOVER

He bites my chin and then licks me until he reaches my lips, then he devours me. Kisses and fire all mixed together. I bite his lip and lick his face as well before I kiss him again.

We fuck hard, unforgiving, hating each other.

And it's the best sex I've ever had in my life.

Even if I may have fucked up my back.

Even if I have blood under my fingernails from digging into his shoulders.

Even if there is regret.

It was well worth it.

CHAPTER
18

Beckham

Jacinta's lying naked on the floor, her bare back to me and her ass perfectly on display for my viewing pleasure.

We fucked all night.

Until we passed out on the floor.

I rub my eyes and sit up, resting on my elbows to admire her as the sun shines in through the window.

She is, quite honestly, stunning.

The last person I thought that about is dead.

She makes a noise as she moves, and I reach for the throw rug and half cover her with it.

"You're still here?" she asks, her eyes not opening.

When I don't answer, she rolls over to look at me, going straight to her back, putting her tits on perfect display for me. And what incredible tits they are.

Standing, I find my trousers and pull them on. "I'm leaving," I tell her, reaching for my shirt. I glance down to find an amused expression on her face.

"You're running. It's cute. But it's fine, Beckham." Jacinta sits up, a little smile on her face. "I want you to run. You should have last night." She stands, the blanket I put over her drops to the floor. "This..." she waves between us, my shirt in my hand, my trousers not fully done up as I stare at her, lost, "... is only sex. And you know what? For once, I'm okay with that and don't want a single thing more from you." She pouts her lips. "You are an ass, and you would make the worst partner ever. But your dick?" She glances down at my cock and smirks, then licks her lips. "Well, he and I, we have come to an understanding."

"Is that so?" I ask.

"Oh, very much so." She chuckles, her laugh hypnotic. Jacinta leans down until she is almost face-to-face with my cock, and I look down at her, my brows scrunching together. "Haven't we, little man?"

"Did you just call my cock little?"

She gives me a slow laugh, then rolls her eyes before she walks, still naked, to the kitchen. Her incredibly small kitchen. Actually, the whole house is tiny. My closet is probably the size of her house. "He doesn't take kindly to those words," I tell her.

She peers back over her shoulder, her hair flicking as she does. "Is that so? And what do you plan to do about it."

When I don't respond or make a move, she turns and goes back to making herself a coffee. I pull my trousers back off and stalk toward her, pushing my naked body against hers from behind.

"Does he feel so little now?" I ask.

She turns, so her body is still touching mine, with a can of whipped cream in her hand. She shakes it and squirts some into her mouth, swallowing before she licks her lips.

My cock bounces at the sight.

Fuck, it's been hard from the moment I woke up next to her.

"Maybe I need a closer inspection."

I pull back, and she shakes her can of cream before squirting it all over my cock. She bends down and licks it off before taking me into her mouth.

Fuck.

Fuck.

Jacinta's head moves, and the can drops to the floor as she grips my balls in one hand, the other at the shaft of my cock, then she starts moving in a perfect motion.

I never stay the morning after having fucked

someone.

Is this what I've been missing out on?

I pull her off my cock and cup her ass, lifting her so she sits at the edge of the counter. She grins at me as if she knew what I was going to do and opens her legs so when I step in between, I can slide straight inside her.

"Maybe only a little, little," she says, which in turn makes me push in more forcefully, making a scream rip from her throat. It's a good scream. One of pleasure, not pain. Because she leans forward and wraps herself around me as I fuck her sweet little pussy.

I've never enjoyed breakfast more.

We're back on the floor—it seems to be a common theme. Jacinta gets up first this time, checks her phone, then addresses me, "You need to go," she says as she heads to what I am guessing is her bathroom. "Thanks for the sex. Show yourself out," she calls before she disappears through a doorway.

Getting dressed, I follow the sound of running water. I find myself in a small bedroom with an even smaller bathroom attached.

She steps out of the shower and her eyes find mine. "Why are you still here?" No woman has ever asked me that. Not ever. Usually, I'm the one asking that question. "My son is on his way home, so it's time for you to leave now." She drops the towel and puts on a bra before she pulls on clean panties. "I'll see you at work on Monday, Beckham," she snaps when I haven't moved.

I'm lost in my own head trying to work out why I'm still standing here when she's clearly ready for me to leave. My head snaps in her direction and I smirk once I come back to reality. "Thanks for the fuck. Call me when you want to go again." I'm already walking out when I hear her voice carry through the door, "Don't count on it."

I chuckle as I leave and get straight into my car. While I'm reversing out, I see Glenn standing outside of his house.

Fuck.

He waves, and I stop.

"It's good to see you," he says. I simply nod in response. "You know I would love if you come inside."

"That's not going to happen," I tell him, my eyes finding the window I used to sneak through all the time. I lost my virginity in that house. That house holds way too many memories—mostly good—but I've grown, and the last thing I want to do is go back down memory lane.

Glenn taps his hands on my door to gain my attention. "Jacinta is a nice girl," he says, smiling and stepping back. "Have a good day, Beckham."

I pull away, wondering what I'm going to do about the employee whom I like to fuck.

CHAPTER
19

Jacinta

"So..." Rylee starts. Oliver runs into the house and straight to his room to play on his PlayStation.

"Yeah?"

"When did my brother leave?" Her eyebrows shoot up. "Is this a thing, or not really a thing? Because I saw the way he was with you and know it's not a first-time thing," she finishes.

"He left, and it's nothing more than what it is."

"Well, I just want you to know I approve. I've seen the type he's usually with, and believe me, I approve." She pulls her bag higher on her shoulder as she turns to walk out. "Not that you need my approval... I'm just saying. He isn't as bad as you would think, I mean. He's pretty amazing and highly supportive. If you need someone to cheer you on, he isn't it, but if you need someone to tell you exactly how it is, he's your man."

"Must be nice having people," I say, and her smile drops. It's then I realize how depressing that sounds.

Rylee lays a gentle hand on my shoulder. "You have people, whether you want them or not." She winks. "I know you said your parents died, but you don't have any other family?"

"No, none. I am an only child, the same as my parents. And their parents died when I was eleven. So... no, no one else."

"Well, that just proves how resilient and strong you are that you've gotten so far by yourself. But you know we're family, right? You need something... you come to me." I nod, and she gives me a cuddle before she leaves.

I shut the door and lean against it.

I never had what she has.

I'm not used to sharing burdens.

When my parents died, I had just turned eighteen and found out I was pregnant with Oliver. I tried coming back to be with Anderson because surely, he would want his son in his life. I had no one, and my hopes were high.

But they were demolished.

And I soon realized I am the only one I can depend on.

I loved my parents, and they meant the world to me. They gave me as much as they could without spoiling me, and they showed me endless love and support.

It's the way I plan to raise Oliver.

They would have loved him.

I wipe a tear from my eye and go to his room to see him playing. He may look like Anderson, but I'm thankful he isn't *anything* like him.

"It seems I may have overstepped my boundaries." I stop at that voice on Monday morning as I walk into the office building. Archie rushes into the elevator with me, hits the button for Beckham's floor, and looks straight ahead. "I wanted to apologize if I came off..." he turns his head away from me as he tries to think of the correct words to say, "... harsh. Scary." He smirks, and that action by itself is scary, and I try hard not to recoil.

"You weren't. It's fine. You're simply looking out for him when in reality, everyone should look out for their own feelings around Beckham. He doesn't care what he says or who he hurts."

"This is true." Archie softly chuckles as the door to the elevator opens, and he exits with me.

Beckham's office door opens, and Beckham stands there, eyeing both of us before his gaze locks on Archie. "What the fuck are you doing here?" he barks.

"See, he's a wonder with words."

I smile and head off to sit at my desk.

"I need your help with a deal," Archie says. Beckham motions to his office and Archie walks straight in. When it's just the two of us remaining, Beckham turns to me. "You're late," he snips.

I check my watch. "No, I'm on time, as usual."

"You are meant to be here when I am, so... you're late." He pivots and walks back to his office, shutting the door behind him.

An hour passes before Archie exits and gives me a small smile on his way out.

"Jacinta," Beckham yells.

With a sigh, I slide on my heels before I walk into his office. When I get there, he's focusing on his computer.

"I need the files for Archie's account. I want you to sort them and bring me everything from the last two years." I nod and walk out, going straight to the filing room. I find the files straight away. There is a massive note on the front warning that they're for Beckham's eyes only. I take a seat on the filing room floor, sorting through them until I get the ones I want.

Someone coughs above me.

"Why the fuck are you on the floor?" I look down at the piles of paperwork scattered all around me. Most of our files are on the computer, but Beckham prefers to have physical ones too, in case the computers crash. I was told his father taught him that.

I don't even bother with an answer, just push my hand up in the air toward him and hand him the files he wants. When he takes them, I go back to sorting the ones that are left.

Beckham is good. All of Archie's money looks legit. But from what I've heard, it is anything but.

"Do you plan to get off the floor anytime soon?" he asks, reminding me he hasn't left yet. He's still standing there waiting for me.

"Yes, I do. But not until I have this all back in order." I don't even raise my head when I speak to him.

"What are you doing in here?"

We both turn to Shandy, who's standing in the doorway. Beckham pushes past her and out, leaving me sitting on the floor with Shandy watching him go before she looks back at me.

"What is going on with you two?" she asks.

"Nothing," I say, smiling.

"Yeah, well... I know that's a lie. Look, you got something delivered and it's on your desk." Confused, I put the last of the files away neatly and stand.

"What is it?"

"Flowers. Big ones, too. So, tell me, who are they from? Because we both know Beckham doesn't do flowers."

Brushing my hands down my skirt, I make my way back to my desk. When I approach, I see Beckham standing there staring at the flowers. When he notices me, he strides straight into his office and shuts the door, with not a care in the world.

"They sure are beautiful," I murmur.

"And expensive," Shandy comments.

MY CRUEL LOVER

There is a card amongst the blooms, so I pick it out and open it.

This is to start a new slate.
I would like to meet my son.

With a quick shake of my head, I drop the card to the floor.

That's a no.

No way.

Never ever!

Who does he think he is? He can't send me flowers and expect to see his son.

Anderson is *not* a good man. He hurt Rylee—almost killed her. And threatened to take Oliver away before I had even given birth to him.

Flowers don't make up for things like that. Not at all.

Prison couldn't have changed him that much in such a short time.

"If you plan to throw them away, can I have them?" Shandy asks, staring at me.

I pick them up and hand them to her. "They're all yours."

She smiles. "Thanks. I had a date Sunday and have another tonight. She's going to love these."

"Glad I could assist," I say as I sit back down.

"Jacinta."

"Hmm?" I look up at Shandy, and her eyes fall to his office behind me. "You're doing okay, right?"

"I'm fine, really."

She nods, happy with my words, and walks off.

I don't see Beckham the rest of the day, which is actually surprisingly hard since he is my boss. When I leave, I don't even bother saying goodbye. I pick up Oliver and go straight to my house. As soon as I close the car door and Oliver runs inside, I see Anderson again. No car this time, just walking down the street.

"You shouldn't be here," I tell him.

He looks me over, and I feel dirty. Filthy.

"My mother is asking about him now."

"Your mother agreed to no contact," I say, which makes him grind his teeth.

"She doesn't agree anymore."

"It doesn't matter. She isn't his mother," I bite back.

"No, but she is his grandmother. Did you get my flowers?"

I look back over my shoulder to see Oliver is

standing at the door. Anderson notices the direction of my stare and then looks as well.

"Go back inside," I yell.

Anderson watches Oliver, but he listens to me and retreats inside.

"I could give you a nicer place to live than this." He examines my house and turns his nose up at it.

"I'm fine with how I live, thank you," I say back to him.

"Did you get the flowers?" he asks again.

"I did."

"And you like them?"

"No. Don't do that again. Especially not to my work," I snap.

"I assumed it would be better than me coming there." He focuses again on my house.

"You should leave." I step back, car keys in my hand.

"Why do you look afraid of me?" His head drops to the side as he assesses me. "I would never hurt you," he says.

"Is that what you said to Rylee?" I ask.

And I shouldn't have. It's taunting him. But I know what a liar he is.

He licks his lips, and his hands go to his sides.

"You are nothing like her. I never loved you like I loved her, Jacinta. You were a piece of ass who just happened to get pregnant and have my baby. Now, to say I would have hoped it was her would be an understatement, but my mother is telling me time and time again that I should be in this kid's life. And I'm starting to believe her. We don't want him to turn out like you now, do we?"

"Leave before I call the police," I say, stepping farther back.

"Just so you know... you can't keep a child from his father or his family. Because that's what I am... what my mother is. Family." He smirks and turns. A shiver goes through my entire body, and now I remember why I ran after I had Oliver—the threats that came from that family.

I immediately call his father. "Your son was just here."

"Are you okay?" he asks. It's something my own father would have asked me. Somehow, I hold back the tears.

"Yes, he just said your wife wants to see Oliver. That they have rights."

"I'm going to talk to my lawyer. Don't interact with them again."

"Leo, he's your son, though."

"Yes, and I also am not blind to what kind of man he is. You have my grandson, who I know is an awesome kid. Who is being raised by a damn good mother. You see where I would rather put my support?"

"Yes," I say almost in a whisper, glad to have someone, anyone, in my corner as powerful as he is.

"If you see him again at your house, call the police, Jacinta."

"I will." I hang up after saying goodbye and go inside, wiping my face clean before I do.

CHAPTER
20

Beckham

"You've been an ass for the last two weeks," Shandy says as she sits on my desk. "And it's been two weeks since my night out when I saw you leaving with an incredibly sexy assistant. What's happened since then?" she asks, crossing her arms over her chest.

"Do you have to be sitting on my desk?"

She scoffs as if I have offended her. "Is the sky blue?" she asks. "Of course I do."

"Well, get the fuck off. I'm sure I pay you for more than sitting around annoying me."

"This is true, but it is the highlight of my week to walk in here and do this. And some weeks when I miss out, it just ruins everything, you know what I mean?"

"No, I don't, but I will once you leave."

She huffs and kicks off her heels before she brings her feet up on my desk and crosses them before she turns and faces me. My desk is big, but that doesn't mean I want to throw her out any less.

"She got flowers a couple of weeks ago, did you see that? I took them," she says smugly. "My new girlfriend loved them."

"I'm sure she loved stolen flowers," I mumble back, paying her hardly any attention.

"She did. She thanked me real good, too. Ate my pussy like it was her last meal." I give her a bored look, and she winks. "Have you had any pussy lately, Beckham?"

"What the fuck do you want?" I almost yell at her.

"To see what your plans are for dinner?"

"Nothing. Now go."

"Good. I need a date. My date canceled, and I made a reservation, and I'm starving. Come. Please?"

"If I say yes, will it get you off my desk?"

"Yes, and what's more, I won't annoy you for a whole month," she adds.

"Yes. Okay, I'll come. Now, get off so I can fucking finish."

She stands, slips her heels back on, and waltzes to the door. "I'll be back at six. Be ready."

"Get out, Shandy."

"Yeah, yeah." She shuts the door as she leaves, letting me finish my work in peace.

"Why isn't your new toy here with you?" I ask Shandy.

"I told you, she canceled." She orders a bottle of wine and looks back down at the menu. "Plus, you pay for dinner, so it's a win-win for me, really."

"Yeah, you get something out of this, and I get nothing."

"Well, not exactly! You get my company. That's a bonus if I do say so myself." She puckers her lips and places the menu down.

"Yeah, you would say so, wouldn't you?"

"I would. Now, what's the most expensive thing on this menu since you're buying?"

"Beckham." Noah's standing there. He turns

to Shandy, says hello, then faces back to me. "Didn't expect to see you here." Noah is engaged to my other sister, Rhianna. Rylee's twin.

"I dragged him out," answers Shandy.

Noah nods at her response.

"Rhi here with you?" I ask, looking past Noah and not seeing her.

"No, actually." He motions to a corner table. "I'm here for business. But I'll see you over the weekend, right?" I nod my agreement and follow him with my eyes as he takes a seat at a table with an older man. I recognize the guy straight away—Anderson's father.

"What're your plans for the weekend?" Shandy asks as the waiter comes back.

We place our orders, and she gets her bottle of wine.

"Archie has a thing going on," I reply.

"Oh yes, I've heard about his parties. You should take me one time."

"No," I answer straight away. Archie's parties, well, they are not for her. Archie's parties are not for many people, actually.

Shandy leans in. "I've heard how dirty they are. Archie has a reputation, you know." She winks.

"Pity you like the pussy. You two could be a

perfect match," I say, picking up her glass of wine and finishing it. A familiar figure walks past us. She doesn't stop or even notice us. But I recognize her. I would recognize her anywhere.

"Umm... was that Jacinta? And is she really going over to sit with Noah?" Shandy says loud enough that the people next to us can hear.

I don't answer her as I watch Jacinta sit down with them, her hands in her lap as they start talking. Anderson's father places his hand on her shoulder, and she taps it before she pulls her hands away.

What the fuck is going on?

"Who were those flowers from?" I ask Shandy.

"Anderson."

"Is she—" The words stop when I see her scan the restaurant. Her eyes skim past me, then come straight back when it registers it's me.

"Well, seems she sees us now. Wave hello."

I do no such thing, but Shandy does. Jacinta waves back then glances at me before she turns back around, giving them her full attention.

"You got it *so* bad," Shandy comments.

"I have nothing."

She rolls her eyes, throwing her head back. "How often do you lie to yourself?"

"As often as I want," I say back to her.

"Well, I'm excited to see how you lie yourself out of this one." She picks up her glass, smiling over the rim.

"Hey, sorry I didn't come over sooner," Jacinta says, leaning down to kiss Shandy's cheek. Jacinta offers me a small smile and remains standing.

"It's no problem. Where's Oliver?" Shandy asks.

"Kids' club here at the restaurant. I have a few things to finish, then I'll be picking him up."

"What is it you need with Anderson's father?" I ask.

Jacinta's hazel eyes shoot to me and narrow. "He is Oliver's grandfather, and he's been helpful with things."

"Okay. Well, maybe after you're finished, you could come over for a drink?" Shandy asks as the waiter brings over our food.

Jacinta steps back as our plates are placed in front of us. "No. I have to get going." She looks back over her shoulder, then turns back to give us a smile. "Enjoy your weekend, though."

As soon as she walks off, I turn back to my food. Shandy has her elbows on the table, her hands under her chin as she watches me.

"Why are you staring at her like that?" she asks, and the grin she is sporting is not missed by me.

"Like what?" I pick up a piece of steak and chew like I don't care what her answer is going to be.

"Like she's that steak you're eating."

"Eat your food and shut up, Shandy."

She pulls her elbows down and starts on her chicken. "I'm just saying, I know you. And you got it bad for the little green-eyed bandit over there."

"Her eyes are hazel, not green."

"See... the fact you know that makes me believe even more you've got it bad."

I shake my head at her words then finish my meal. Shandy tells me about her date, amongst other things.

"You leaving?" Shandy asks as Jacinta walks past us again.

She stops briefly. "Yeah, good seeing you both. I'll see you on Monday."

"Hmm, what did you do to her?" Shandy asks.

"It's time we get going. Get your shit."

"But I want dessert," she whines.

"I'll give them my card. Order your dessert, but I gotta go."

"Whatever." She waves me off as I hurry out of the restaurant. As I exit, I see Jacinta straight away, leaning down and doing up the buttons to her son's jacket.

I hang back, and when she stands, I slide my hands into my pockets as she turns to face me. "Beckham," she says.

"Hey, Beckham." Oliver waves at me and Jacinta gives him a confused look.

"You know Beckham?"

"That's Winter's favorite uncle, Mom. Beckham is the coolest." I smirk at his words. Kid's got taste.

"Yes, the coolest," she says sarcastically, then opens her car door so he can get in. "Was there something you needed?" I look down to the closed window and back to her.

"Come back to mine."

She clutches her purse in her hand tightly. "No."

"Why?"

"Because I have my son."

I lean down and knock on the window, and Oliver winds it down.

"Hey, I have a heated pool and an Xbox. You want to come and hang out at my place with Mom?"

His eyes go wide at my words, and he nods his head eagerly.

"That was pure evil," Jacinta hisses under her breath.

My lips go up in a smirk. "Follow me," I say as I head to my car.

As I pull out, I check the rear-view mirror, and low and behold, she follows.

CHAPTER
21

Jacinta

I should have expected something like this. I mean, really, I should have. But as I clutch my purse to my chest, I just can't. He strides around so casually, grabbing a few towels, then coming back out. Oliver is ecstatic and already down to his shorts, then he jumps into the heated pool. But the smile on his face is well worth the pain I am feeling at being forced to be here.

"Get undressed," Beckham instructs as he reaches for his own shirt and pulls it over his head, so now he's standing in front of me in just a pair of shorts.

He looks way too good.

"I have nothing to wear." He passes me the shirt he was wearing, and I take it. "Now you do. Get in." He spins and dives straight into the pool.

We are in an apartment building, but he has a rooftop pool all to himself.

Who the fuck has that?

Beckham does, that's who.

I stand and pull my shirt off—it's not like he hasn't seen me naked before—and slide his shirt on. Then I take off my bra underneath, followed by my skirt. The shirt is long enough that it covers just below my ass. When I finally get into the pool, it's warm and oh so nice.

Oliver is floating on his back as he tells Beckham all about school.

Beckham listens attentively.

Which surprises me.

He smirks at me from the other side of the pool.

I sit on the step and watch them both.

An asshole with my son.

Yet somehow, Oliver chats to him like he's his best friend. Tells him all about the video games he's obsessed with, and Beckham even joins in on the conversation.

"Mom, can we stay the night? I want to play Beckham's Xbox. I have a PlayStation, and all my friends have an Xbox, so I want to try." Before I can say no, that we cannot stay at this man's house who makes me feel things, Beckham speaks for me, and I'm unable to say anything.

"Of course you can stay. I'll put the Xbox in Winter's room for you."

Oliver fist pumps the air before he dives under the water. I turn, glaring at Beckham.

Beckham makes his way over to where I am on the step and sits next to me. "Why do you look so uncomfortable?"

"This is weird," I tell him under my breath, making sure Oliver can't hear. Though, he's too busy diving for toys and then throwing them and diving again to pay us any mind.

"Why? Because I want to fuck you in my bed tonight?" His hand is under the water and comes to rest on my thigh. He slowly moves it up until he is near my entrance. The only thing stopping him right now from going in is that I am wearing panties.

"Stop," I say with a heavy breath.

"You don't sound like you want me to stop. The vein in your neck is pulsating and your breathing has picked up. Looks to me like you want this as badly as I want to give it to you."

I turn to face him and his smart-ass mouth. "Do you bring many women back here?"

He touches my hair and brushes it behind my shoulder, breathing me in. "None. You are the first."

"I'm hungry," Oliver says.

Beckham squeezes my leg, then pulls away. "Let's get you fed, then." Beckham steps out of the water, and Oliver follows him gladly, not even bothering to ask me if I'm coming. I dive under the water when he's gone to release a scream before I come up and climb out of the pool.

Picking up one of the towels and wrapping it around myself, I grab my clothes and go inside. I don't see them straight away, but I can hear Oliver's laughter as I make my way past the overly large living room to a bedroom with the light on.

Beckham is sitting on the floor, a towel around his waist and a game controller in his hand, as Oliver eats a packet of chips on the bed.

"You have to jump here." Beckham does so with his controller, and Oliver pays close attention.

"This is a beautiful room," I say, looking around.

"It's Winter's room," Oliver says, still looking at the television.

"Okay, got it?" Beckham asks him.

Oliver nods happily and takes over the game.

"He can't play all night. He needs rest," I tell Beckham when his hands grip my waist and he pushes me out the door.

"Oliver knows the TV is set for an hour, then he has to go to bed. He has his own bathroom there if he needs it, don't you, buddy?" Beckham says, not looking back, just staring at me as he says the words.

"Yep," he shouts. Oliver is too entranced in what he's doing.

Beckham shuts the door with one hand still on me. "What do you think we should do?" His eyes roam my body suggestively.

"Nothing," I answer back. I go to turn toward the kitchen, but he pushes me in the opposite direction. It's dark until he claps his hands, and soft lighting comes on. "You plan to seduce me?" I ask, giggling. Facing the room, there is an enormous bed in the center. And when I say enormous, I'm not joking. I've seen king beds, and this one is way bigger than your average king-sized bed. The room itself has one black textured feature wall, where the other two walls are a lighter gray. There are wall-to-ceiling mirrors along one wall, which I am sure hide an ensuite. The bed is covered in a black with silver pinstriped duvet, and there are large cushions at the bedhead. At the end of the bed is a studded black leather bench. There is a huge television hanging on the wall opposite the bed. The whole area is bigger than my entire home. It's ostentatious, but not in a bad way.

"I've already seduced you. Now it's all about getting you into my bed." I step away from his touch and wander around his bed. I can tell which side he sleeps on because his phone charger is there.

"Why such a big bed?"

"I like my space."

"You don't like to cuddle?" I ask while attempting to hold back my laugh.

"No, I do *not* like to cuddle."

"Pity. I love to cuddle. Especially naked. When you get so close that you can just slide..." I open my mouth to an O and snap it shut, "...

straight in. It's one of my favorite positions." I smirk at him.

"Is that so?"

"Very much so," I tell him, dropping the towel and then pulling my panties off before removing his shirt and climbing into his side of the bed. I pull the duvet over me and lie on my side.

"Well, I'm all for experiments," he says before removing his pants. He comes to the bed and gets in the same side as me, pushing me over until we both fit. His hand runs down my side before it gets to my ass and travels farther down until he grabs the spot directly under my knee and hooks it over his waist. That same hand then moves between us until he finds my clit and rubs just a little. He brings his fingers up and holds them in front of my mouth. "Lick."

I do as he says and taste myself. He smirks and then licks his own fingers, the ones I just licked and puts his hand back between us so he can rub my clit again.

I start moving and arching into him, and he bites his lip, his dark eyes turning heated before he leans over and kisses my exposed neck.

Feeling anything for Beckham is not something I ever wanted to do.

It wasn't meant to happen.

How did it even happen?

I shake my head when I feel him at my entrance. He hikes my leg up higher on his waist and slides inside me. I pull myself closer until no air can squeeze between us, and he starts moving.

Lips, hot and heated, continue to kiss me, stealing them as a thief does jewelry in the night. I let him steal my diamonds because I know in return, he will make something out of them.

And it will be magical.

Until it isn't.

I push him away so his kisses can stop thieving, and when I do, he pauses. I catch my breath and push him again, so he rolls on to his back, and I go with him. Now on top of him, I push my wet hair over my shoulders and start moving my hips.

Beckham lightly strolls his fingers down my back until he reaches my ass and slaps it.

I move faster, and his hands grip and help me move even faster.

To walk away would be smart.

To not get involved would be smarter.

I have managed to do so up to this point.

We have managed to work together at the office, but now it feels different. Everything feels different. Especially when I see him staring at me the way he is now. It makes me feel so many emotions. And none of them I should be having for my boss. Of that, I am sure.

"Stop that." My hands grip his face, and I push it away so he can't stare at me any longer. I close my eyes as I come, and he keeps on moving me, pulling my head down so my face is directly in front of him.

"Kiss me."

And I do because it's better than the alternative.

When he comes, he holds me to him, not letting me go.

Eventually, I say, "I need to use the bathroom," and try to get off of him.

He lets me leave, but his gaze tracks me as I grab his shirt and head to the ensuite through the glass doors and throw it over my body as I shut the door.

The shower has two heads and is four times the size of mine. I use the bathroom and wash my hands, then splash water on my face.

Telling myself I can walk out there, I do.

When I open the door, the light is on and Beckham isn't there, but then I hear, "He's asleep." Beckham's standing in the doorway with a towel wrapped around his waist.

"You checked in on Oliver?" I ask.

"It's adults I don't like. I love kids," he says, walking back to the bed. "You have a good kid." He throws back the duvet, loses his towel, and slides in, holding the cover open for me. "You look good in my shirt but much better with it off."

"No more sex. I can't risk Oliver walking in. I don't even know why I allowed it the first time," I say while looking at the door.

"Get in bed, Jacinta."

When I reach the bed, he grabs hold of my hand and pulls me down, so I land next to him. Then positions me so I'm in a spooning position on his side of the bed. The whole other side of the bed remains untouched.

"This is a big bed," I say, nodding. "You can move over if you want."

He harrumphs near my ear but doesn't move.

"This is going to have to stop," I tell him. "We can't keep doing this."

"Hmm," is all the response I get.

I close my eyes and wonder what my life would be like if I never met Anderson.

I would not be here.

I wouldn't have Oliver, which I do not regret for one second.

And I would have never met Beckham.

His hands tighten around my belly, and I hear the soft snore that follows soon afterward.

What a conundrum he is.

CHAPTER
22

Beckham

Jacinta and Oliver are gone when I wake.

But did I expect anything less? No.

The kitchen is clean, and not a trace of her remains anywhere.

My head hits the counter as I lay my hands on it, wondering why I am feeling like this.

While I am leaning over and thinking, the front door opens, and in walks Rylee. She eyes me as she walks straight over. "What is going on with you two?"

She couldn't have known about last night.

"Shandy?" I ask.

She rolls her eyes almost to the back of her head. "Of course. She is my best friend. Now, tell me, do I have to watch for anything? Is this a smart move?" she questions. "She works for you, and more than that, she also has a son."

"She was out at dinner last night with Noah and Anderson's father."

"Anderson wants to see Oliver, and she doesn't want him to. Anderson's father hired Noah to get something more permanent in place, as what they have isn't working."

That makes sense.

"She has a kid, Beckham," Rylee says again. "Do you know what you're doing?"

"No. But I don't need you to tell me either. If that's the only reason you're here, then you need to leave."

"You sound like August. He told me to stay out of it, but I care for both of you. And, well, after Paige..." I grind my teeth at her words, "... you haven't wanted anyone since her. It's been six years, Beckham."

"I've been with multiple women," I bite back, stepping away to the fridge and pulling out a bottle of juice. "Do you want their numbers?"

"That's not what I mean, and you know it. You haven't had any kind of relationship with any of them. They are nothing more than fuck buddies."

"That's by choice, or should I say... *my damn choice,*" I tell her.

"No, it's not. It's because you can't handle anything more. And that's fine, it is your damn choice... but remember one thing, if you keep going with Jacinta, you will need to be careful. Feelings might develop, things might change."

"Don't you have a kid to raise?" I bark.

"Yeah, yeah." She waves her hand at me. "If Shandy asks to go with you to one of Archie's parties, tell her no. I've heard about them, and she for sure does not need to go to that."

"Maybe I should take August." I smirk.

She stands taller and points her finger right in my face. "You will do *no such thing,* brother." She turns and walks to the door, then looks over her shoulder directly at me. "I'm blocking your number today. Call tomorrow." She walks out and shuts the door.

I check my phone and see Archie has sent me the time for the party.

"She's a pretty little blonde thing, don't you think?" I look in the direction he's pointing.

"Go then..."

He nudges me. "For you, Beckham... not me. You need it more than me."

Bringing the glass up to my lips, I take a small sip while I watch everyone and then reply, "I'm fine."

"Unless you are fucking that sweet ass from your office, you aren't."

Ignoring his comment, I scan the room. I've been to a few of Archie's parties. He holds them mainly for his criminal clients. It's somewhere they can do what they want and fuck who they want under the protection of his home.

He lives out of town, and his driveway is basically its own street, complete with security cameras, so he knows if anyone is coming down it, and that includes the police.

This gives them enough time to make sure people can leave easily via the back way out of the property. Everything is perfectly timed, so if there are any issues, everything goes like clockwork.

"What about that brunette?" He nods to another girl who's walking around wearing nothing but body paint.

When I look more closely, she has handprints slapped all over her body in bright red and pink paint. I raise an eyebrow when I glance back at him. "Archie, fuck off."

He throws his head back and laughs. No one annoys him. They know better. He throws these little soirées to gain their trust. He needs their confidence so they will delegate business his way, and while his mandate might be one of confidence, Archie needs to ensure these people know their anonymity is of paramount importance to him.

It's one of the reasons Rylee would never want August to attend.

Everyone who attends these events belongs in prison, and August has already been inside. Therefore, if something did go wrong, he would be thrown back inside, and that's not something Rylee is prepared for.

Plus, there's pussy.

Fuck, there's so much pussy here.

Rylee would not want August anywhere near this shit.

My phone starts ringing in my pocket, but I ignore it as Archie keeps on pointing out women who he thinks will interest me.

"The best way to get over someone is to get under another. Surely, you have heard that saying?" Archie keeps going on and on.

My phone rings again, so I eventually pull it out of my pocket to two missed calls from Jacinta and a few from Rylee. Before I can put it back, Archie's phone starts ringing, and he shows me the screen before he answers with, "Favorite sister. When are you going to leave your boy toy and run away with me?" he says, smiling. Then his face drops, and he hands me the phone. "You should probably take that."

I give him a puzzled look and take the phone from him.

"Beckham. Beckman, can you come? Now?"

"What's wrong?"

"Oliver is missing, and Jacinta is a mess. I can't calm her down." I hear a scream in the background and then Rylee whispers, "Please come. I don't know what to do."

As I pass the phone back to Archie, he stands. "What's going on?" He takes his phone and slides it back into his pocket. "Do you need me to do anything?"

"No, just..." I look around and reach in my pocket for my keys, then look back at him. "Maybe... I'll let you know."

"Do you want me to drive?" I hear him say as I walk toward my car.

"No." I don't know if he hears me, but I don't really care as I get in my car and go straight to her.

Cars are parked out front of Rylee and August's home. I spot Glenn straight away, his hands on his hips in his uniform—he means business.

"Beckham," Glenn says my name, and August, who is standing with him, turns to face me.

"What happened?" My gaze flickers to the house as the front door opens, and I see Jacinta standing there, her eyes red and puffy.

"Anderson is unreachable. His mother picked Oliver up from school today..." August says.

Jacinta makes her way closer to me, and I take a few steps in her direction. Once we reach each other, I pull her in. She grabs hold of my shirt. Jacinta is sobbing. I can feel her chest going up and down as she breathes heavily, but her voice is silent.

"You haven't tracked her down yet?" I ask, my eyes flicking to Glenn, who's watching us interact.

His eyes lift to mine. "No. We have applied for a warrant, but it takes time. And so far, the child isn't listed as in danger, just with his grandparent."

"She stole him," I state categorically.

"Anderson was with her, so technically, his father did," Glenn replies.

I rub her back. "I can find them."

Her sobbing stops, and she pulls back to look at me. They all go silent and focus solely on me.

"How can you find them?" August asks.

I ignore him and look directly into Jacinta's sad eyes. The hurt punches me in my chest like a bullet going straight through from seeing her like this. So damn broken.

I like her.

A lot.

I always knew that fact.

But now? Now I *know* it.

"I can find them," I repeat, pulling my phone out of my pocket and stepping away so Glenn can't hear me speaking. Jacinta stays where she is, her hands hugging her body as I call Archie.

"I need you to track this car and number."

Archie doesn't ask any questions. He has one of the best hackers I've ever had the good fortune of meeting on his books. He's so competent, even the authorities haven't found out about him yet. I hear him talking with his accomplice, and not more than a few minutes later, I hear, "Found him. Texting you the address."

As soon as the address comes through, I hang up, walk to my car and get in. Just as I am about to pull out onto the road, my passenger side door opens, and August slides into the seat.

"Rylee will kill you."

"Drive," he barks, and so I do.

August should have killed Anderson, and right now, I bet he wishes he had.

"You're joking, right?" August asks as we come up to Anderson's childhood home. "Jacinta came here. The police came here," August says.

"It's where my source says he is, and believe me, he will be right." I get out, and August follows.

"Fuck, I hate him," August grumbles.

A car pulls in behind us, and I see Archie get out and lean against it, his gun casually held in his hand against his thigh as he smirks at us.

"You sure you know what you're doing?" August questions, referring to Archie.

"Always." And it's true, I am always in control.

The only person I seem to lose control with is *her*.

Even with Paige, I was always in control, always on my game.

But Jacinta, well, she's different.

Looking at the house, you would think no one is home, but then, just the slightest movement from behind a blind gives the game away.

"Kick it in or knock?" August asks with a smirk.

I walk to the front door and kick hard. It flies open on the first try. As soon as we step inside, there he is, flying to his feet.

"Anderson," August growls, and Anderson's eyes flick to August, then back to me.

"You kicked my door in," Anderson says in disbelief.

"Where the fuck is Oliver?" I demand.

"Isn't he with his mother?" Anderson says, but the smile gives it away.

You can't fix stupid.

Anderson is the definition of stupid. If you could look it up in the dictionary next to his name would be the words 'a stupid moron.'

"Look, last chance before I smash your fucking face in."

Anderson just laughs. "You..." he eyes me up and down, "... would never want to get yourself dirty," he says, then turns his attention to August. "If the threat came from you—" I don't let him finish. Two steps, and my boot meets his face. When I pull my foot away, his face is coated in blood, and he is flat out on the floor.

"Do you ever learn?" August says.

"How dare you." We hear a screech and turn to see Anderson's mother standing there with Oliver in front of her. Her hands possessively clutch him.

But what gets to me is the fact she has Oliver positioned in front of her. Is that for her protection? That she would use a child for her own personal security as a safeguard against getting hurt?

"You come into my house and assault my son?"

"Oliver," August says. "Your mom is missing you. You want to go home?"

Oliver nods his head fast and goes to move, but she holds him in position.

"That can't happen. We are all getting to know one another. Oliver wants to stay with us."

"No, he does not. Now, remove your hands from him," August warns.

I slowly move until I am behind Anderson, who is still on the floor, clutching his nose.

"I think it's best you listen to August," I tell her, and her dead eyes fall to me. I reach forward and give Anderson's nose a kick, making him scream in the process.

"Don't you think your family has done enough to ruin our lives already? This is my grandson. I will be keeping him."

"He is not your son. And if you wish for *your son* to see his next birthday, you *will* remove your hand from Oliver so he can go to August." I raise my hand again, her eyes fall to her son, and she lets Oliver go. As soon as August has him, he leads Oliver outside. I wait until they're gone before I reach for Anderson, pulling him up by his shirt.

"Archie is outside with a gun. He is ready to come in here as soon as I leave," I seethe in his face.

His eyes go wide at the mention of Archie's name. "I had nothing to do with it. It was all *her* crazy idea. She told me I *had* to do it."

"You really are a sack of shit, aren't you? A worthless, gullible, imbecilic piece of shit."

He doesn't say anything in return.

"Drop him." I feel something sharp touch my side.

"I wouldn't do that if I were you," I warn.

"You obviously do not know the lengths I will go to to protect my son."

"And you *obviously* don't know me," I reply, as the click of a gun being cocked sounds close by. I hear the knife drop to the floor, and

Anderson looks at Archie, who's casually standing in the doorway, gun at his side and a smirk on his face as he takes in the scene in front of him.

"Thought you were taking your sweet ass time," he says.

"It wouldn't be appropriate to hit a woman, would it?" I ask, pushing Anderson back to his couch and hitting his broken nose one last time for good measure.

Damn asshole.

"I can keep a secret ... so if you want, go at it." Archie grins.

I turn to face Anderson's mother, and her eyes are now wide with fear. I lean in until I am a hair's breadth away from her. "You come near Jacinta or Oliver again... I may just let Archie use his gun on you. Because you know..." I wipe my hands on my suit, "... I don't want to get my hands dirty with scum like you."

CHAPTER
2 3

Jacinta

The relief to have him in my arms, holding me with his little hands wrapped around my waist, is indescribable.

He is my life.

I love him more than life itself.

Everything I do, I do for Oliver.

We stay like that, him cuddling me, until Oliver pulls away, smiling.

"Can I play with Winter now, Mom?"

I nod, wiping my tears away as Shandy comes and sits next to me on the porch. She pulls me in with a one-arm hug and squeezes. "You'll be all right. You got this."

And I believe her.

I do.

"What do you plan to do about the Beckham situation?" she asks.

August came back with Oliver in Beckham's car but without Beckham. I didn't ask questions because I was so happy to see Oliver home safely.

Fine with not a scratch.

Healthy.

Happy.

I simply wanted to love on him.

"What do you mean?" I ask, confused.

"Well, you two have had something going on for a while now. Do you plan to continue that? Will you be happy being an every-now-and-then lover?"

"No," I say truthfully.

"I didn't think so, and I'm afraid that's all you may ever be to that man. I mean, don't get me wrong, he's different with you than any of the others he's fucked. But Beckham is almost incapable of affection or love." She pauses then takes a deep breath. "Unless you are his family or a friend. Are you friends?"

"I don't even know the answer to that question."

It's true. I'm not sure what we are. And I stopped assuming in relationships after Anderson. You know, considering he was already in one and got me knocked up.

"Well, it seems our boy has arrived." Shandy stands and heads inside.

Beckham gets out of the car, and Archie nods to me before he drives away. It's dark, and the street light shines on him as he strides up the driveway toward me. Even though his eyes are as dark as a stormy night, I can feel his gaze penetrate me. Soaking into my bones.

"He's home," is the first thing Beckham says.

"Thank you," I say in reply. Standing, I reach out and wrap my arms around his neck. He doesn't hold me back at first, simply lets me hold onto him, and I'm thankful that he does.

A few seconds in, his hands come around my waist and he clutches me to him, so close I feel all of him.

I pull back, knowing what I need to do. Closing my eyes, taking a deep breath, and then opening them again, I say breathlessly, "I think we should stop seeing each other." He would have heard the words croak as they left my mouth.

The doubt as I said them.

The undeniable uncertainty they scream.

But I mean each and every word.

I need to focus on Oliver and me.

Just the two of us for now.

"Your focus is on you and your work. And as you said before, I'm just a fuck. I need to focus on Oliver, so something like this can never happen again," I tell him.

He still hasn't spoken.

Not one single word.

"Beckham."

We turn to Oliver, who's at the door. He runs down the steps and into Beckham's arms. Beckham's eyes find mine, his mouth in a thin line, he's breathing deeply.

"Winter said I wasn't allowed to play on her Xbox again," Oliver says, pulling back.

"Of course you are," he replies.

"Okay, I have to tell her that." Oliver runs off back inside with a smile on his face.

"I..."

Do I take my words back?

I know he sees the hesitation in my eyes.

When I turn back to him, the look in those dark eyes is going to haunt me, of that I am sure. They will give me nightmares for years to come—dreams that will be impossible to stay away from.

He bites his lip, his two top teeth pulling as he studies me.

Why is he such an asshole?

My eyebrows pull together.

Why do I want him so much?

My jaw clenches.

Even when I know I shouldn't, I still need and want him.

"You made your bed. Now you have to lie in it," he replies, and the smirk that follows is cruel. Oh, so cruel.

Why does he have to be my cruel lover?

My head hangs, while a pained expression shows on my face. I simply can't help it. So I take a step toward him, but he shakes his head and steps back, not wanting me anywhere near him.

Well, that hurts more than I care to admit.

But I'm someone who's familiar with hurt. It's basically my middle name. A stray tear leaves my eye and runs down my cheek.

Beckham's watching me with those dark storm-ridden eyes, but he hasn't walked away yet. *Yet,* being the operative word.

"I..." I'm at a loss for any words to give him. How can you tell someone you think you love that it's simply not going to work? Especially after you told them you no longer want them and that it will never work.

Not only because we were never right for each other in the first place, but because I'm too broken to want his love.

Oliver is all I need.

Or so I keep telling myself.

Beckham has proved time and time again how fucked up we are together. It just took time for me to see that fact as well.

"We were never official. You are my employee, and that's how it will stay," he says deadpan.

How has a year passed that I have been working for him? A year of ups and downs and cruel words followed by touches that make me forget everything in my world around me. Every word that leaves his mouth can be led away with one single touch.

We were never exclusive—that was made perfectly clear.

Just something that happened.

Something that kept on happening despite us trying to stop it.

We should have stopped it.

He's my source of confidence, but also for my self-loathing. And I stand here helplessly in the night as I watch him walk away. Knowing full well, I have caused my own hurt, my own devastation.

Even if I know it's for the best.

I will not be that girl again. I will not be someone's second choice or fuck buddy.

But even more so, I can't be with him because he still loves Paige.

I want to be someone's first.

I deserve to be someone's first.

I want someone to look at me and see only me. Not wish they were seeing the person they really want to be with. Be the touches they crave and wish were someone else's.

I will *not* be that girl again.

"He left?" Rylee asks, standing in the doorway. She watches her brother pull away, his car the only noise that can be heard in the distance. "I have made you up a bed. You should stay the night. Oliver has climbed into his bed and is almost asleep."

"Did you hear?" I ask.

She looks down to the floor. "I heard enough."

"Do you think what I did was stupid?"

"I think it's up to you who you choose to give your heart to. No one else should be a factor in that decision."

Charges were pressed, but I don't know if they will stick. Anderson's father has been a great help, and he assists me where he can. And because of that, I am letting him pick Oliver up next week instead of going to afterschool care.

I simply don't trust that Anderson's mom won't come back and try something like that again.

And Beckham? Well, it's been almost a week, and he's barely said two words to me. He barks orders, then he disappears. That's the extent of our interactions.

Friday afternoon, I have to stop at the restaurant to meet Noah to sign some more paperwork, and when I arrive, I see Beckham sitting with a female opposite him. She leans in and smiles at what he says, her body language indicating she likes what she sees.

I know that look only too well.

I like what I see too.

I scan the room to check if there's a way around them, but it's impossible. I will have to walk directly past them. Not looking their way, I walk by their table and try not to look in his direction. It's hard when I can feel his eyes on me, soaking me in.

"Jacinta."

I stop. My heels halting me at the sound of his voice.

"Do you plan to ignore me?"

I mean, it sounded like a good plan in my head.

Plastering on a fake smile, I turn to face him and his companion, who's smiling up at me.

"I'm in a rush. Sorry."

"Noah isn't here yet. Why don't you have a seat and wait? I'm having dinner with him after you two finish anyway."

"Is that why you're here?" I ask. My eyes can't help themselves, and they fall to the woman. She's beautiful, very much so. Dark mahogany hair falls down over her breasts as she sits there, legs crossed. And her red lipstick begs for someone to pay attention to her lips.

I look down at my own outfit, and it's then I realize perhaps I should have changed.

I'm still in my work clothes, but I didn't have time to change into something else. I got home from work, cooked Oliver's dinner for when he comes home, then slipped on my shoes and left again.

Beckham pulls out the seat next to him and nods for me to sit.

"I really shouldn't be interrupting your evening. I'm happy to go and wait for him over there." I nod to a spare table.

"It's no bother. Sit," he commands.

So, I do.

"Hi, I'm Amy." She offers me her hand, and I take it.

"Lovely to meet you. I'm Jacinta... I work with Beckham."

"Nice."

"And we used to fuck," Beckham says, then turns to face me. "Isn't that right?"

I narrow my eyes at him and then purse my lips. "I'm sure your date here does not want to hear about your conquests," I snap.

"Amy isn't my date. She owns this place, and I can assure you she doesn't care who I date because she prefers to fuck Shandy."

Oh.

I smile when I turn to face her. "Shandy and I are good friends," I tell her.

"Nice to know. How about I let you two talk?" She stands and saunters off, leaving me sitting with Beckham. He picks up his drink and sips it before he swirls it in the glass, the rocks clattering around and his eyes firmly on me.

"How's your week been?" I ask, trying to make some sort of conversation.

"Small talk? Is this what you have come to? You don't want to know how I've been sleeping? Who I've been fucking?"

"You've been fucking someone?" I ask, surprised.

Then instantly, I shake my head.

Beckham smirks as if he expected that answer.

Asshole.

"I can fuck *you* if that's what you want?"

The chair next to me is pulled out. "Sorry, I won't keep you long, Jacinta. Can you please sign these, and you can be on your way." Noah hands me the forms, and I pull my eyes away from Beckham's blazing stare and reach for the pen.

As soon as I'm finished, I stand. "Goodnight," I say to them both.

Noah tells me the same.

Beckham just stares after me as I leave.

CHAPTER
24

Beckham

"Why don't you tell her?" Noah asks as I watch Jacinta walk out the door.

"Tell her what?"

"That you love her."

Placing my glass on the table, I wave for Amy to come over. "Because I don't."

"You do," Noah replies, smiling. "It's fun to deny until you get to that place where you have denied it for so long that she also no longer wants to believe you."

"We aren't the same," I tell him. Yes, he lost his first love, but we aren't the same. Noah is a good man. He is kind to my sister, and she needs that because Rhianna is the spitfire of the family, and she can always stand her ground. Even against a lawyer.

"No, you're an asshole, and I'm not," Noah says with a grin as Amy comes over to take our orders. "So, you met Jacinta. What did you think?" Noah asks.

"I think someone has a crush." And we both know who she means. She's talking about me, and I scoff at her words.

"Shouldn't you be making me a drink?"

"Shouldn't you be chasing after the pretty little brunette?" she bites back and turns to leave.

"You should, you know. Go after her, I mean."

"She made it clear we aren't going to work."

"She also had an eventful day that day, or did you forget that fact?"

I turn to face him. "How is Oliver?"

"I haven't seen him, but the girls talk every day, and Rylee told Rhianna that he's fine. Jacinta was more a mess about the situation." Noah picks at the breadstick in front of us.

My eyebrows pinch together, and I stand to leave.

Noah smiles, knowing full well where I'm going.

Like a fucking stalker, I sit out the front of Jacinta's house because that seems to be what I have become.

A stalker.

It's been two hours since she left the restaurant. I drove around before I finally pulled onto her street and then in front of her house.

I watch as she opens her front door, stands there, and stares at me.

Getting out of the car, I make my way to her. She stands taller once I reach her. She's dressed in a lace nighty, and her hair is up in a messy bun.

She looks tired.

But so unbelievably hot.

"Beckham—"

"Is Oliver asleep?" I ask, cutting her off.

She nods, and that's all the permission I need before I step up to her and kick the door shut behind me. My hands circle her waist and lift her up. She comes easily, her legs wrapping around me before I walk backward to her room. When I enter, I shut the door quietly, holding her up with my other hand so as not to wake Oliver before I lay her carefully on the bed.

Her hair falls from the bun and cascades all around her before I grasp her nighty and lift it over her head.

"Why are you here, Beckham?" she asks when I kick off my shoes, then undo my shirt.

"I thought that's obvious," I reply, looking down at the hard-on in my pants. I remove them, and her eyes fall to my cock before they return to mine.

"Is it just sex?" she asks on almost a whisper.

"No. But you know that already," I reply.

Lying down, covering the top of her, I brush her hair back.

"You despise me," she says.

I kiss her neck.

"Beckham!"

I look into her eyes, and I can see the flicker of gold in them. *How did I not notice that before?* "Hmm," I hum, not wanting to talk right now. My body wants other things. Moving between her legs, I feel her entrance, and she spreads her legs wider, giving me as much access as I want.

"I'm your employee," she says through heavy breaths.

"That you are. But right now, you are anything but my employee, wouldn't you say?" I ask as I reach my hand between us.

She gasps. "Yes. Yes... I very much would."

My mouth falls to her tit, and I take her nipple between my teeth. As I pull on it, she moves her body up, pushing me even closer until she wraps her legs around me.

"Tell me what you want?" I ask, moving to her entrance but not pushing in.

"You."

"How do you want me?" I tease as I move to her other breast.

"In me. Now."

"So demanding," I answer, pushing in slightly.

"So annoying," she grumbles, putting her heels on my ass and pushing me farther into her.

And down the rabbit hole, I go.

Literally.

Hers.

And I will gladly go there time and time again to get lost in a sea of hazel and soft smiles paired with tender kisses.

Fuck.

I'm there.

CHAPTER 25

Jacinta

I wake to Beckham lying next to me. His breathing is heavy as he sleeps on his stomach, one hand cast over my waist, pinning me to the bed. Which I might add, we aren't even sleeping on the right way. I turn my head and check the time. It's still early. I must have gotten only a few hours' sleep, but I have to rise because Anderson's dad is taking Oliver to the circus today to give me a chance to do Mom things while he's gone for a few hours.

Cleaning. Groceries. You name it.

Slowly, I try to remove Beckham's hand, careful

not to wake him as I climb out of bed. I only get so far before his hand catches and pulls me back down. His face goes to my chest, and he holds me to him.

"I need to get up to get Oliver ready."

"Grrr…" There are more words, but I can't figure out what he says. After he's finished speaking, his arm loosens, and he lets me go. I pull away and look down. His eyes are half-closed from sleep, but he is watching me.

"You look hot."

"Not gorgeous? Not delectable? Just hot?" I scoff, reaching for a dress and throwing it over my head.

"No, you look fucking fantastic. So fucking good, I have to stay on my stomach because my cock has other ideas, and those ideas involve you. But because you have to tend to your son, I will keep my words to letting you know you're hot, at least until we're alone and I can ravish your body with my tongue and cock. That any better?" he asks, brow raised, the other one half covered by the pillow. "I suggest you answer and leave before I decide to lock you in here with me and have my way with you again and again."

"You better go back to sleep."

I step out the door and close it behind me. Leaning my body on it, I take a few deep breaths as my hand lays on my beating heart.

I think…

… I love him.

I've never felt this way for a man. Ever. I would never allow one to come into my house and sleep under the same roof as me if I didn't trust him.

And I do trust him.

And I don't trust many men.

Managing to move, I get Oliver's breakfast ready before he comes into the kitchen, rubbing his eyes and going straight to the table where his bowl sits.

"Is Beckham coming out for breakfast?" Oliver asks, looking up from his iPad.

My eyes go wide at his words, and then I blink a few times. My words are caught in my throat.

"Sure am. What you cooking me?" Beckham asks, stepping out fully dressed.

How did he do that so fast?

Beckham sits next to Oliver and grins at my shocked expression. He leans over and scruffs the top of Oliver's head. "Oliver here ran into the room this morning, so I put him back to bed," Beckham explains.

I look at Oliver. "What was wrong?"

"He needed water," Beckham answers for him. "Easy fix."

Oliver looks back down to his iPad as I place

another bowl of cereal in front of Beckham. He smiles as he takes it, then leans over to watch whatever Oliver is doing. I head to my bathroom, pausing to glance back at them—both their heads in sync as they stare at the screen.

After fixing my face and hair, I go back out to find Beckham cleaning the kitchen as Oliver is getting ready.

"You don't have to do that," I say as Beckham pauses and peers at me over his shoulder.

"I used it... I can most certainly wash it." He doesn't understand what that small gesture does to me. I'm so used to being alone that having someone choose to help me warms my heart.

"Did you love him?" Beckham asks, not looking my way.

"Who?"

"August. Did you love him?" His dark eyes find mine, and his hands remain in the sink as he washes the last dish. He's waiting patiently for me to answer.

I didn't think he would ask me that, actually. I didn't think Beckham would ask me much about my life at all. I didn't think he would care enough to ask such questions.

"Yes," I say.

His chest rises and falls at my words. He turns back to the dishes and continues.

"But not in the way he loves Rylee," I finally say. "I'm starting to see that I loved him, yes, but I was never really *in love* with him. Probably because his heart always belonged to her, and I was just a fixture in waiting until she came back."

"I'm pretty sure I love you."

My heart stops at his words.

My eyes go wide.

I can't move.

How do you respond to someone who says that, who has never given you anything but their body before? Never given you one ounce of anything but anguish.

I open my mouth and shut it.

He isn't facing me, but I know he's waiting for my response.

The doorbell rings, and I make no move to answer it until it rings again. Then I walk past him to the front door, opening it to Leo, who's standing there. He smiles at me as Oliver runs over. I don't like to bring up Anderson and his mother around Oliver, so I keep my mouth shut in regard to what's happening with them or if he's heard from them. Leo steps into the house to grab Oliver's bag and flinches when he sees Beckham wiping his hands on a dishtowel.

"Beckham..." he pauses. "Nice to see you."

Beckham nods and goes back to cleaning.

Cleaning? Who is this man, and what has he done with the man who barks orders at me?

"We should be back tonight. The circus is a little later in the day, then I am going to take him to the park to run around a bit. Then I will feed him before we come back if that's okay with you?"

"That will be lovely," I say, smiling. I bend down to kiss Oliver, and he hugs me, then runs over to Beckham and cuddles him as well. Beckham pauses as Oliver wraps his arms around him from behind and taps his hand with a smile on his face.

"Have a good day, kid." I shut the door when they leave, and when I turn, he's right there in front of me.

Beckham's lip curls and I'm reminded of what a cruel man he can be.

But he isn't that way with me right now.

No, he looks as if he's planning all the ways he could eat me.

"I'm sure you have plans today," I say, my hands flat against the door.

He steps up closer until I can feel his breath on my face. "I'm sure I do."

"Hmm..."

"And you can accompany me. Like in one hour, I'm meant to be at my mother's house for lunch. And you're coming."

"I don't think that's a smart idea," I say breathlessly.

He doesn't seem to care though as he leans in and grips my chin softly, lifting it up so I have to look straight into his eyes. "It is. I'm going to introduce you as my girl."

I suck in a quick, shallow breath. "That's *for sure* not a smart idea."

"Why? Do you plan to fuck other men?"

I shake my head.

"Do you plan to date other men?"

I shake my head again.

"Well, I think it's a splendid idea then." Beckham leans in close, his lips ghosting on mine. "Now, I think..." he looks down at his watch, "... we have an hour to kill. What do you say we shower?"

"I'm already clean."

He licks my neck, and I'm so shocked by it that no words leave me.

"I disagree. Now, come, let me clean you." Beckham turns, gripping my hand, and pulls me with him.

I can't help the giggle that leaves my mouth.

How did I manage to bag this man?

Beckham is literally unlike any other man I have ever met.

As soon as we reach the shower, he turns to me and pulls my dress off in one fell swoop, then he takes a step back, his eyes roaming my body. A part of me wants to cover up, but with the way his eyes are devouring me, I know he wouldn't like it.

"I think you are the most beautiful woman I have ever met."

The way he says it leaves no room for argument. Beckham removes his shirt and jeans, then he turns on the faucet in my small shower. I wonder how we're both going to fit in there. But as he steps in over the lip of the bathtub and stands there, he offers me his hand, and I gladly take it and step in after him.

The water washes over him, and he moves the showerhead so it falls between us, then he grips my hips pulling my body closer.

"What if we don't work?" I utter in a whisper, almost talking to myself.

"But what if we do?" he replies a lot louder, hands sliding down to my ass and lifting me until I wrap my hands around his neck and my legs around his body. "I think I'm going to fire you anyway."

"What? Why?" I ask, shocked.

He chuckles and kisses my neck. "Rylee can give you another position. Having you outside of my office, knowing I can call you in and bend you over my desk anytime I want, is far too tempting. It's best I remove that temptation."

I push on his chest, which is hard considering he has me held up against the wall. "If you fire me, you will not get a piece of this ass ever again. You hear me?"

"Yes, ma'am." He nods, then moves me, so I'm in the perfect spot for him.

"I've met your mother already. Do I have to come? I have so much I need to do."

"Yes, I know, but you haven't met her with me. And I want to introduce you as my girlfriend. And what do you have to do?" he asks, making my eyes shut as I slide down on him.

I completely forget what he said.

Until he snaps at me, that is.

"Jacinta." My eyes snap open, and Beckham is nibbling on his bottom lip. It pops out before he speaks again. "What do you have to do?"

"I need to clean and get groceries."

"I'll handle it. We can do groceries on the way home."

I go to speak, but he shakes his head. "Now shut up, so I can fuck you."

And that's exactly what he does.

Makes me scream.

Smacks my ass.

Tries to make me call him 'daddy.'

And then brings me to that land of pure fucking pleasure.

Beckham has a marvelous cock, no doubt about that.

CHAPTER 26

Beckham

Jacinta's fidgeting. I smack her hand away, and she laughs.

"You look beautiful."

"Did you really call your cleaner?" she asks, her laugh gone now as we walk up the steps of my parents' house, where she's never been before.

"Yes. She's on her way. I pay her generously and have had her for years. She's good. I trust her implicitly."

"I don't need a cleaner."

"Your shower says otherwise." I smirk.

She blushes.

"That's your fault. I told you the shower wasn't going to be big enough."

"I'll buy you new soap, washes, and whatever else I might have broken." I may have accidentally knocked them over and spilled them all over her floor. Her bathroom is incredibly small. It's like a closet in comparison to mine.

And I had plans to fuck her, so nothing else mattered at the time. Therefore the mess I left behind was probably more than it should have been. Still, my cleaner will make it sparkle before we return.

"It makes me uncomfortable when you throw around your offers."

I pause and turn to her. "What offers?"

Her perfect brows pinch together. "Things that cost money. I know you're used to it, but I'm not. Please stop offering things, especially stuff that costs money I don't have," she says, as the front door opens.

My mother is standing there. Her gaze falls to Jacinta. She assesses her, then moves back to me. "You didn't tell me you were bringing anyone, Beckham. You know better than that."

Ha.

She thinks she can play me like she does the

girls. Well, she should know better than that. I stopped being manipulated by her a long time ago.

"Nonsense. I don't need to inform you. We both know you have more than enough food. Now, let me introduce you to Jacinta. No rude comments or talking down to her. I am not Rylee. I will straight up leave and not come back."

My mother forces a smile. "I'm not rude," she snaps, then looks at Jacinta. "Your son? He's not here?"

"No, he's with his grandfather today."

"Wonderful. The girls are inside already." My mother steps back to let us enter, and I kiss her on the forehead as I show Jacinta to the living room. Rylee smiles and offers her a drink straight away as Rhianna smirks, simply watching me.

"I'll be back," I lean down and tell Jacinta.

She nods and takes the seat next to Rylee as I walk out. I find my mother opening a bottle of wine as I enter the kitchen. "I love her."

My mother's brows rise at my confession. "Do you, though?" she questions.

"I do. I see her differently than I have ever seen a woman in my life. I think about her all the time. She is my first thought each morning and my last every night."

"It could be infatuat—" my mother attempts to say before I cut her off.

"It's not."

"She's below you, you know that. Surely, you know that?" She lifts her glass of wine and takes a few sips. "A kid. No house. Been married. Gosh, what else is there?"

"Is that all you see?"

She scoffs and shakes her head. "No. Do you really want to know what I see?"

"Enlighten me, Mother," I egg her on, crossing my arms over my body, taking that please educate me with your damn thoughts stance.

"You won't leave?" she asks. "I mean… you did ask."

"No, now tell me."

"Fine then." She takes a deep breath. "I see a woman who's not good enough for my son. My son who has a lot at stake and something for her to win. You may have been smart with women in the past, but you aren't with this one. What? So you're going to marry her, and then when she leaves, she takes everything you have worked so hard for with her, and she runs away with the next man in line who can give her more than you can." She takes a deep breath, and I grind my teeth at her words. "I know girls like her. Lost, looking for love, and shown money. Now that's all she wants. It's why she went after Anderson… money. How much is she getting from that family? Considering how well off they are, I'm sure she would be getting enough to not work a day in her life. Have you seen under her bed? Do you really know all her secrets? It's quite evident you don't. All I'm saying is watch her, get to know her first. Gold-diggers are good at hiding where they stash their cash."

My mother's eyes fall on something behind me, and I turn.

Jacinta's standing there, her eyes glassy as she looks at me.

"I think we should leave."

My mother offers her a small wave as Jacinta turns and walks away.

"You said you wouldn't leave," my mother reminds me.

"That was before you turned into an A-class bitch."

"Beckham," my mother calls out after me, but I don't even pause, walking straight out the front door. Jacinta is heading down the driveway.

"Jacinta."

She doesn't stop. Her feet keep up the rapid pace she's set, and I have to jog to catch up with her. When I finally reach her, I grab her shoulder, but Jacinta shrugs me off and keeps going.

"Will you stop?"

She finally does, in her tracks, and whips

around to face me. Tears are falling down her face. "I've put up with a lot in my life, Beckham. *A lot*. But I am *not* going to put up with someone who cannot defend me, who sits there and listens to those awful comments your mother threw my way. I get it. I do. She's your mother. But if my mother, rest her soul, said anything like that about you, I would have corrected her the minute the words spewed from her mouth. But no, you encouraged her. I heard it all, and you never once defended me. I want to go home, and I would very much like you to not follow. I'll see you Monday. Please don't stop by again."

"Let me drive you home."

"I've called a cab. I can pay for that myself, so you don't have to worry about my gold-digging ways. Thank you very much." Jacinta turns and proceeds down the driveway, and my feet stay stuck in the gravel as I watch her leave.

"Beckham." It's Rhianna, and she's looking at the end of the driveway as I watch Jacinta get into a cab, and it pulls out into traffic. I've been standing here waiting and watching. "You should know better than anyone to protect people you love around our mother."

I turn to face her, and she smiles sadly.

"You've watched us go through it, and now you're the golden child."

"She left," is all I say.

Rhianna's forehead scrunches as she comes closer then touches my shoulder. "Give her time if that's what she wants. But not too long… if you want her, that is." She squeezes, releases me, then turns, and walks back inside the house where I was brought up.

Allowing myself to breathe for a few moments, I eventually turn and step inside. My mother is standing at the door, waiting for me.

"That was so wrong," I tell her. "And worse than that, I let you say it. I didn't defend Jacinta at all."

"Because you know what I said is true."

"No, it's not. If you took the time to get to know her, you would know that." I close, then open my eyes, trying to get rid of the vision of Jacinta's hurt face, then I spin around and walk to my car. Over my shoulder, I say, "You fuck up all your relationships. How our father has managed to stay with you, I will never know."

She gasps. "Beckham."

"You better think of a way to make that shit up to Jacinta. Fuck! Even try to get to know her because I plan to keep her around for a long time."

"What about Paige?"

"Mother."

Both the twins are standing there now, their eyes on our mother as she says the name of the woman I once loved who died.

"What about Paige?" I ask.

"You can't replace her. That woman... that woman is nothing like her."

I shake my head. "I don't want another Paige. I had Paige, I loved Paige, and I have mourned her."

And it's true, I did love her, I have mourned for her, but she is no longer here, and I can finally see that. Paige is never coming back.

"It's not Paige who holds my heart, Mother. I don't even know if adult Paige and adult me would have worked. We worked when we were younger because we loved each other. But the me I am now only has eyes for one woman. Do you understand?"

"It's a mistake."

"It's not. You won't be seeing me again until you fix this."

"I'll come to your work. You won't be able to avoid me, Beckham. I am your mother."

I smile at her threat. "And Jacinta will tell you I'm not available." I get into the car, not bothering to argue with her anymore. She's caused enough trouble for one day.

"Didn't expect to see you so soon," Archie says, sliding out from underneath his Shelby Cobra, which he refuses to drive or sell. I know for a fact it's worth upwards of one million, but he says progress takes time. Well, this one has taken a shit load of time. "You blow it already with the girl?" He chuckles, wiping his hands on his dirty jeans.

I take a seat in the chair near him and open his fridge, which is always fully stocked, and pull out a beer for myself and throw him another.

"Mother. I took Jacinta to see her."

Archie laughs and shakes his head. "Why on earth would you think it would be a good idea to take Jacinta around your mother? You know who she is. What she is. Shit! It's been what for Rylee? She had August's baby, and your mom still didn't want August or the baby."

He has a point. There's no doubt about that.

He rubs his jaw. "Unless you went in knowing she'd be like that and did it on purpose. Could you be sabotaging on purpose?"

"No."

"Are you sure?"

"The pain... that I put there." I shake my head. "Time. I have to give her time," I say.

"No woman wants time. If you really want her, you would already be there, not here." He rolls back under the car and I leave.

CHAPTER
27

Jacinta

Beckham's cleaner was here when I arrived home. I attempted to ask her nicely to leave, but she nodded her head as if she didn't understand me.

Once she finishes though, she speaks perfect English and tells me she'll see me next week. All I can do is nod from where I lie curled in a ball on my bed as I listen to her pack up and leave.

How could he stand there and let his mother trash-talk about me like that?

Just after he told me he loves me.

This relationship is not healthy.

Not good.

I'd call it fragile.

I had an example of a great relationship growing up. So, how I have managed to pick these bad eggs, I will never know.

Anderson being the worst one of them all.

But I never felt this pain in my chest the same as I do with Beckham.

This longing, this kind of heartache. The emotional tightness, the shortness of breath, and the anxiety when I think about him have me feeling almost lightheaded.

My phone pings and I want to ignore it. But Oliver isn't with me, so when I check it and see that it's not Beckham, I'm hit with relief but then overwhelming sadness.

It's Leo letting me know he won't be back for a while, but he sends a picture of Oliver through. I thank him and rise from the bed. I need to do at least one thing on my list before my already ruined day becomes any worse.

As I arrive at the shops, my phone starts ringing. I see Beckham's name flicker on the screen when I look down.

Nope.

Not answering.

Not a chance in hell.

Going in, I reach the chocolate aisle and grab more than I usually would.

Budget, I think.

Fuck my budget.

Chocolate is going to be the answer, along with sad movies tonight.

My phone rings again, so I silence it and move on.

"Do you plan to ignore me for the rest of the day?" I jump, my hand falling to my heart and the milk splattering all over my feet when it somehow slips through my fingers.

Shit.

Damn it all to hell!

I look up into his dark eyes, and his hand grabs my cart as it almost runs away.

"I asked for space," I tell Beckham as someone comes over with a mop.

I apologize. Beckham does not.

"And I gave it to you." He looks down at his watch. "Four long hours."

"You should leave." I pull away and try to maneuver around him, but he blocks my path.

"Okay, we need to talk," he says.

I place my hands on my hips. "Talk, then move it. I have things to do."

His hand reaches up and scratches at his brow as his full attention focuses on me.

I used to feel scrutinized under someone's gaze but now, not so much.

"I shouldn't have let my mother speak about you in that way."

"No, you shouldn't have. Why would you even bring me to that place if all you wanted to do was hear the bad words your mother has to say about me?" I half yell. People walk by and stare, neither of us caring. All that exists is us in our own small bubble right now.

I used to like that bubble when his hands would roam my body, and his dark stare would penetrate me.

"And for the record, Leo sends me checks. Big ones to help support Oliver. Basically, what he would have given his son. But I don't cash them. Hell, I don't even open the envelopes. I didn't ask him to do that. He just does. I don't want your money, Beckham. As far as I am concerned, you can take your cash and stick it up your mother's ass." I push past him, taking my shopping with me. He lets me, and I get to the checker before he's behind me again.

"I'm not sure what else to say to you. I told you this morning that I have fallen in love with you. Then this afternoon is ending like this."

"I would defend you, Beckham! If someone loves you, they defend you."

He scratches his face. "I'm learning, Jacinta. It's been a long time since I cared for someone other than myself."

I nod and push forward while the checker who's scanning my items watches us. I smile, and she looks down, blushing. Clearly, she's heard everything we just talked about.

I pay and walk out, but he follows.

"It won't happen again," he says from behind me.

And I kind of believe him.

When I turn to face him, I have to remember to breathe. "I need to get home," I say in defeat.

"I want to come," he states, but I don't answer him. Instead, I get in my car and drive home. When I get there, Beckham pulls in behind me. He walks over, reaches for my bags of food, and follows me inside, placing them on the counter. "Forgive me," he pleads.

"They hurt, just so you know. Those words hurt me."

"I'm sorry." He wraps his arms around my waist and pulls me to him. "I'm sorry," he says again, both hands coming up to my face, cupping me so he can see me. "I'm sorry," he says once more, this time leaning down and kissing me. Soft, tender, and dare I say it...

... with love.

"I've loved someone before," he says between kisses. "But never this way. Not like this. Not where I can't function." When I catch my breath at his words, I simply nod. "You are ingrained in me now. I'm very selective, Jacinta, and I choose you. Do you understand, I choose you?"

"You love me," I say.

He smirks, those gorgeous lips lifting before he nods. "Fucking truth, I do."

"And you are sorry?"

"Yes. I will not be speaking to my mother again. We will *not* see her until she apologizes."

I grip his hands around my face. "Don't do that. She's your mother. You only get one. Trust me, I know this."

"Tell me about them... your parents," Beckham says, lifting and placing me on the counter, wedging his body between my legs as he waits for me to answer. "Tell me everything about them. So I can understand you."

"They were each other's first loves. Only loves..." I pause. I remember how my father used to make my mother angry, but moments later, he would play music and dance in front of her until she smiled. He was an awful dancer. And she loved to dance. "I look like her," I tell him.

"Well then, she must have been one fucking looker." I smile as he pulls me closer and kisses my mouth. It's not a soft kiss this time. It's a hard kiss. An, I'm sorry kiss. And I take it because I love him too.

Even if his mother is an ass.

Lips so tender push against mine, hands so rough search my body, for what, I'm not sure. Breaths so rapid have trouble catching mine.

"Ignore it," Beckham says, his hand sliding up my skirt until he reaches my panties.

I smile as the knock comes again and then huff. He pulls away, putting distance between us, so I can jump off the counter. I wipe my mouth, which is covered in us.

"It's Oliver," I tell him, heading toward the door. Upon opening it, Oliver barrels into my legs, and Leo stands there smiling, holding onto his bag.

"He's been excited since dinner to come to see Beckham," Leo says, looking behind me at where Beckham is now standing.

"Well, we shall not disappoint." Beckham follows Oliver to his room to show him all the things he got today, and I turn back around to Leo.

"Anderson doesn't want to know Oliver. It was all his mother's doing," Leo says.

"She's left. She is no longer in the country. She met a man. It was quick and now she's moving to Paris." Relief washes over me. "She just informed me, and I wanted you to know." I nod, smiling.

Glancing over Leo's shoulder, I see Glenn getting out of Leo's car.

"Did Glenn go with you?" I ask, confused.

"No, I picked him up on the way. He's lonely, and well..." He looks back at him, and Glenn offers me a small wave before he meets us on the porch.

"Nice to see you, Jacinta. I hear my boy is here." As he says the words, Beckham appears. His hand slides to my waist while his brows pinch in confusion.

"Are you two..." I ask, not sure how to finish the sentence.

"I think we are," Leo says, smiling back at him. "Glenn isn't around when I have Oliver, but I was hoping, given time, he could get to know him as well."

"I'm happy you're happy." And I am. Glenn is an amazing guy who lost the only person he ever loved. His daughter, Paige, and Beckham's first love. And from what I have heard, he hasn't been the same since. And today, he is standing in front of me smiling.

I can't wait to tell August.

"I'll tell August," Glenn says, looking at both of us. "I'm glad to see you back, Beckham, I always knew you were bound to be a father. A good one, too. You have always had that kind of soul."

I turn around to look at Beckham to see his reaction to those words.

"Goodnight, gentlemen," Beckham says.

Glenn smiles, knowing full well how Beckham is and nods to me before he walks back to the car.

"Next weekend still okay?" Leo asks.

"Yes. Why don't we make it a regular thing? He loves hanging out with you. How about every second weekend he spends one night at yours?"

Leo beams proudly and leaves with a, "Thank you."

Beckham shuts the door. "Now, where were we?" he asks, pushing me up against the door and sliding his hand up my skirt.

"Oliver," I remind him.

"Occupied with my phone."

That *will* keep him busy for a while.

"What about photos on your phone? You

don't have any naked women on there, do you?"

"One day, yes, I plan to photograph you naked and have it as my screen saver."

I smile at his answer as he lifts and carries me to my bedroom. He throws me on the bed, and we are quick with removing our clothes. Once we're both naked, he comes over and sits. I climb onto his lap and wrap my legs around his waist.

"I love you, too," I say to him as he reaches for his cock between us and positions it so I can slide down.

"I already knew." He smirks, then leans forward to bite my lip.

"I could be lying," I say, my head dropping back. He takes the opening to bite my neck, then slides his teeth down until he reaches my breasts and bites them too.

"Now that is a lie."

And he's right.

Oh boy, is he right.

"You should make me tell the truth all the time," I taunt him, my body moving against his. I go to say more, but he grips and holds me down on him, stopping any form of movement.

It's torture.

My body wants what his can give and is currently not.

"I'm not lying," I say, and he loosens his hold on me, bites my ear before he proceeds to fuck me until I see stars.

And what magical stars they are.

CHAPTER 28

Beckham

I haven't left Jacinta's house for two weeks. I go to work, then take her home.

I like being around her.

Consumed by her.

She slides her hands up under my arms and hugs me from behind as we get out of the car and walk to her house. As we reach the door, she pulls back and stops.

"Your mother is here."

I turn and see my mother getting out of her car. She straightens her dress, her heels digging into the grass as she walks over to us.

Assessing eyes fall on me, then Jacinta, who's now standing by my side, frozen to the spot.

We haven't spoken of my mother since the incident a few weeks ago. She made no attempt to apologize, so I made no attempt to contact her.

"Did you take a wrong turn?" I ask.

Her head snaps in my direction, and she narrows her eyes. "No, I didn't expect to see you, though."

My brows rise at her words.

"You came to see me?" Jacinta asks, and her hand slides into mine, where I clutch it protectively.

My mother's eyes don't miss the movement as she watches and nods. "Yes, I did."

"What for?" I ask.

"I'm direct, harsh, and sometimes mean." Her nose is pushed up as she says the words. "And I want to take the time to apologize to Jacinta personally for my words."

I turn to look at Jacinta and see a small smile on her face.

"Thank you for taking the time to come over and apologize. I just want you to know, I don't want your son for his money. And for you to think that before you even got to know me... well, it hurt."

My mother's eyes fall to me before she nods. "I understand. My girls always like to point out that I can be quite rude and harsh. So once more, I apologize and will not speak ill of you again. And I'm glad my son has found someone who makes him happy. Like Paige did."

"Paige sounds like a wonderful girl, and I'm sorry I'm not her. But I don't think Beckham would want me to be like Paige anyway."

I look down at Jacinta. "No. No, I do not." I lean down and kiss her forehead.

"You'll start coming again? To family lunches?" my mother asks in a hopeful voice.

"With Oliver," I tell her.

"Yes, nice boy, that kid. Well mannered. You've done well raising him." She turns and walks back to her car and slides in.

"Is your mother affectionate?" Jacinta asks as we watch her drive away.

"No. Only with my father."

"You two are a lot alike, you know. Blunt, rude—" I reach for her at her words, cutting them off as I throw her over my shoulder and carry her inside the house.

Then I smack her ass, hard, for those words.

Even though I know they are true.

"Your tits are getting bigger."

"Oh, fuck off," she says as she looks down at them. Then in one swift movement, she is off and running to the bathroom, slamming the door shut behind her.

With quick steps, I run after her and knock on it.

"Leave me alone."

"What the fuck is going on?" I ask, clearly confused.

Jacinta doesn't answer. Instead, she makes me wait. I lean on the door, and she opens it with a white stick in her hand. Her eyes are glassy, and she looks up at me with wide eyes. She's rubbing her forehead, and there are no words.

"What's wrong? What's that?" I nod to the stick and go to reach for her.

"I'm pregnant." The words slip from her mouth.

It's late. Oliver's asleep, and I am staring at a white stick as if it may grow a head.

"Fuck."

I look up and search her face.

"I'm on birth control. I told you this. So…" She pauses and takes a deep breath. "Whoever thinks they're going to be in that small percentage of where it fails? That was not me." She answers her own question as she walks past with the stick still in her hand and waving it around.

"Move in with me." The words leave my mouth before I have a chance to think about it, and she looks up at me with teary eyes.

"That's your response? Move in with me?"

"Yes. Is it… wrong?" I ask her, confused.

"It's just… when I told Anderson I was pregnant, he asked me how much money I needed to get rid of it." She wipes away a stray tear. "It's a very different reaction and not one I was expecting."

"I'm nothing like that piece of shit."

She hiccups. "I know."

"I hope in a good way," I say. Walking over to her, I place my hand under her chin and make her look up at me. "Move in with me?" I ask her again in a low tone.

"You don't want to live here?" she asks. She hasn't wanted to go back to mine, as she doesn't want to break Oliver's routine. So, I happily stay here. Oliver is a priority for her, just as she is to me.

"Where are we going to put the baby?"

"It could be false symptoms and a false positive test," she blurts out.

"It's not. Your tits are bigger, and you've been more emotional." I wipe her face and lean down to kiss her tears away. "My sister was a bitch when she was pregnant."

"Are you calling me a bitch?"

I laugh. "No, but I've made the decision. You two are moving in with me. I have the room, and Oliver will be happy there. He loves my place, which will now be *our place.*"

"I don't know…" I kiss her to shut her up. "I know what you're doing," she says as I continue to kiss her.

"And what's that?"

"Distracting me," she whispers before kissing me back.

"Is it working?"

"Always," she says, reaching her hands around my neck and pulling me down to kiss me.

"Mom." We both pause as the bedroom door

opens and Oliver stands there rubbing his eyes. "I had a bad dream," he says.

"Book a doctor's appointment, and I'll put Oliver back to bed," I whisper to her. She doesn't speak, but I know she understands me from the slight nod. "Come on, buddy." Oliver is a good kid, and he goes back to bed with no problems after I read him a short story. When I get back to the bedroom, Jacinta is sitting cross-legged on the bed.

I stand at the door, watching her as she stares down at the white stick. She turns her head to me when she notices me standing there.

"You can run. I'm used to men running. Now is your chance," she says in a shaky voice.

"I would never do that to you," I say, walking over and climbing in behind her. "I may be an ass, but I would never do that."

She chuckles, and it's music to my ears. "We're having a baby," she says.

"We are," I confirm.

"Shit."

"Fuck," I say, smiling from behind her.

She turns and lets me kiss her cheek.

"I once described you as my cruel lover. Now... well, you are anything but."

CHAPTER 29

Jacinta

One Year Later

My hands caress his face. Who would have thought he would look at me the way he is, with so much love and admiration? It's a beautiful thing to have someone you love stare at you like that. It's something I will never take for granted.

Beckham's hands touch my flat stomach, now scarred with white lines and ripples. He smirks as he moves closer, his lips finding mine in a frenzy of passionate kisses. Then, like clockwork, the baby starts crying.

"She can cry," Beckham says, and I chuckle because I know what's coming next. He groans as he moves me and touches between my legs, finding me already wet. And just as her screams become louder, he's up and off of me, adjusting himself. "I'll be back. Stay where you are. Do not move."

"I need to shower," I tell him, resting up on my elbows.

He points at me. "Stay." So, I lie back down as he leaves.

I never expected this life, but I am not complaining about it.

Somehow, I found a man who's not only a great father but a great man in general. Well, at least to me, he is. He's still an asshole to almost everyone around him, and most of the time, I have to remind him to walk away.

He's especially standoffish to the mothers who try to talk to him when I'm not with him. He gets a lot of them, a lot of attention, and he's just plain rude to them. But for some strange reason, they keep trying, which confuses me.

I still work for him, part-time. Shandy fills in for the other half, which works out great because anyone else would probably quit, as he is a complete ass to work for.

I hear our beautiful girl, Estelle, stop crying, and know Beckham has it under control. It's so different for me this time around. It's basically a whole new experience.

It's not just me.

I have Beckham this time.

He is the best father, even to Oliver, who asked if he could call him dad.

That broke my heart, just a little, that I had failed him in that department. But Beckham puts it all back into perspective.

Oliver, well, he is the best big brother a little girl could ask for. I feel like I hired two nannies without actually doing it. We moved into Beckham's home, as his place is bigger, and my house didn't have the room to add him and the baby to the mix.

It took a lot of adjusting.

Just like things with his mother.

I'm pretty sure she still to this day dislikes me, thinking I am some sort of gold-digger, but she's a good grandmother, and that's all I can ask for despite her bitchiness toward me.

"You moved."

I roll over to face him. He has Estelle against his chest as he rocks her to sleep. Her eyes are fighting, but they are slowly closing, losing her battle with the inevitable.

"I need to shower."

"No. Wait for me."

"I need to shower," I tell him again. "I have to get ready for work."

"You're fired. Now stay in bed and listen to your boss."

"You may be the boss at the office, but you most certainly are not here." I wink at him, getting up and tearing off his shirt that I like to sleep in.

"That's unfair. No." He shakes his head. "That's just plain fucking cruel. You do know you'll be spanked for this, right?"

I turn around and wiggle my ass at him.

"Now you're simply asking for it," he says as I walk to our very, no, enormously large bathroom. "Mommy is a tease. A dirty little tease who is going to be punished." I giggle as I hear them walk away and step into the shower.

As I am rinsing my hair, I feel hands slide up behind me before they drop farther down to my ass and lightly tap it.

"I warned you."

I turn around to face him. "That you did."

He smacks my ass, not hard enough to make me scream but hard enough to make me yelp and pay attention.

I went through a stage where I worried about him falling in love with another girl. What if he saw another woman and wanted her instead of me?

Then, one night, as I was walking out of the bookstore, he was waiting for me at his car, not paying attention to anyone around him. It was like his whole word was solely focused on me. And I knew then, with certainty, how much he loves only me.

That I was it for him.

As he is for me.

I haven't been sure of many things in my life, but of him, I am.

Beckham's my favorite asshole, and I think I may just keep him forever.

OTHER BOOKS BY
T.L. SMITH

OTHER BOOKS BY
T . L .   S M I T H

Buried in Lies

Distorted Love (Dark Intentions Duet 1)

Sinister Love (Dark Intentions Duet 2)

Cavalier (Crimson Elite #1)

Anguished (Crimson Elite #2)

Conceited (Crimson Elite #3)

Insolent (Crimson Elite #4)

Playette

Love Drunk

Hate Sober

Heartbreak Me (Duet #1)

Heartbreak You (Duet #2)

My Beautiful Poison (Wicked Poison #1)

My Wicked Heart (Wicked Poison #2)

Find all of her books on
www.tlsmithauthor.com